HOLD ME CLOSE

SIOBHAN DAVIS

This edition © April 2026
ISBN-13: 978-1916651203

Editor: Kelly Hartigan (XterraWeb)
Proofread by Courtney DeLollis.
Cover design by Shannon Passmore of Shanoff Designs
Cover design and interior images © depositphotos.com
Formatted by Zsuzsanna Gerhardt of Midnight Readers PR

Note from the Author

This novella is set approximately seven years after the epilogue in *Let Me Love You* and it is not a standalone read. You must read *Say I'm the One* and *Let Me Love You* before reading *Hold Me Close*.

Fair warning – you may need some tissues for this!

Happy reading.

Glossary of Irish Terms/Sayings

The explanation given is in the context of this book. Also includes pronunciations.

Aisling – female Irish name. Pronounced Ash-ling.

Arse - ass

Oisin – male Irish name. Pronounced Ush-een.

Plain sailing – smooth sailing

Tops up (as in wineglass) – equivalent of tops off.

Zip - zipper

Sons pay for the sins of their fathers...

Bodhi and Easton Lancaster O'Donoghue have grown up sheltered from the truth. Until it's time for their parents to reveal what happened and how it shaped the events that came later.

Bodhi is quiet. An intelligent, introspective boy who hides his pain deep inside. Shattered by the harsh reality of the past, he spirals into a dark place where no one can reach him.

Easton loves his brother fiercely and has always been there for him. Despite his own grief and confusion, he tries his best to support Bodhi—even if he seems determined to push everyone away.

Vivien and Dillon knew this moment would come. Yet nothing prepared them for the massive fall-out. As Bodhi retreats, and Easton struggles, they fight hard to keep their family together.

Before history repeats itself and they suffer more devastating loss.

HOLD ME CLOSE

Chapter One
Dillon

"You have the rest," Ash says, dumping the remainder of the bottle of white wine into Viv's glass. "You look like you need it."

My wife arches a brow as she stares at her sister-in-law-slash-best-friend. "Is that your way of telling me I look like shit?"

"Puh-lease." My sister rolls her eyes. "That's a virtual impossibility. You always look stunning, babe."

No truer words have ever been spoken. My wife is a fucking goddess, and she only gets more beautiful with age. I regularly pinch myself. I still can't believe she's mine. That I get to share such an incredible life with her. Viv has given me everything I never dared to dream of, and I love her so fucking much.

We fought hard for our love, and I never take it—or her—for granted.

My heart melts as I look at her, admiring her natural beauty and the elegance she exudes from her every pore. Viv inherited some incredible genes. Lauren, my mother-in-law, is sixty-six and still one of the most stunning women in Hollywood. She has chosen to grow old gracefully, refusing plastic surgery and proudly showcasing the thick streaks of gray lining her jet-black hair. She eats well and works out regularly, and she still has a beautiful figure. Viv's dad is no slouch either. He looks years younger than his seventy-six, and he is fit as a fiddle and sharp as a tack. If they keep it up, they may outlive all of us.

Ash reaches around Jamie to squeeze Viv's arm. "It's my way of telling you you look stressed. You work too hard."

I wish that was all it was.

Viv takes a healthy gulp of her wine as I slide my arm around her shoulders and move in closer to her in the booth. This Italian restaurant is Viv's favorite primarily for the large velvet-backed circular booths that are comfortable and perfect to fit the six of us with ease. It's also tucked away in a quieter part of L.A. and not one of the trendier celeb haunts. No one pays more than a passing interest in us when we come here. The food is also to die for, and they serve this bramble gin cocktail Viv loves.

"I have three words for you. Pot. Kettle. Black." Viv drills Ash with a knowing look.

"The difference is I have one child to look after. You have four."

"And two teenage boys is no picnic," Audrey adds, swirling the wine in her glass.

"Tell us about it," I say, knocking back the last of my Peroni.

"More trouble?" Alex asks, quirking a brow.

"The boys got suspended from school for five days," Viv admits, and I hear the strain in her tone.

Leaning in, I press a kiss to her temple and hold her close, wishing I could absorb all the stress for both of us.

"That isn't like either of them," Jamie says, gesturing at the waiter. "What happened?"

I wait until we have ordered another bottle of wine and three more beers before replying. "Some shitheads at school got their hands on a Saffron Roberts porno, and they printed out stills of it and plastered it all over Bodhi's locker," I explain.

Jamie curses under his breath.

"As if that wasn't bad enough, they taunted him about her, and that's when Bodhi lost it," Viv adds. "He threw the first punch. Then East got involved, because you know he always defends his brother, and it turned into a massive fight in the hallway."

"I hope they suspended the pricks who did this." Alex's jaw is tight, his eyes blazing with the same anger Viv and I felt when we first found out.

"They should fucking expel them," Jamie says. "And Bodhi shouldn't be punished for standing up for himself."

"It doesn't work like that," Alex says. "The school can't be seen to condone any type of violence. If Bodhi threw the first punch, he's equally as culpable in their eyes." Alex knows what he's talking about. Until the twins were born, he worked as a football coach at a local private high school. He understands how volatile teenage boys can be with all that testosterone and aggression flooding their bodies.

"Everyone involved was suspended," I confirm, nodding in thanks when the waiter places a fresh beer in front of me.

Audrey tops up the girls' wineglasses as a waitress appears, depositing our main courses on the table.

"That sucks for Bodhi," Audrey says, lifting her cutlery. "Kids can be so cruel."

"The boys have had to deal with this kind of crap before." Viv twirls pasta around her fork. "But this is a new low. Bodhi isn't handling it well."

That's the understatement of the year. "I have to practically frog-march him from his bedroom to join us for dinner," I say, grabbing a slice of my pizza. "And he has barely said a word to any of us all week."

"He internalizes everything," Viv says. "And that can't be good. I want him to speak to a therapist, but he's refusing."

"You can't force him, sweetheart." I remind her again. We've had this conversation a lot this past week. "At least he's venting some of his emotions through his songwriting. He's been down in my studio most days working on new stuff."

"It's ironic that Bodhi is the one more obsessed with music," Ash supplies in between bites of her ravioli.

"It's not really." Viv pauses eating to reach for her glass of water. "Bodhi adores Dillon, and he's naturally gifted with a guitar. They bonded in those early days over music, and I truly believe it helped Bodhi cope with Lori's loss and the big change in his life when he came to live with us."

"Easton is really fucking talented too," Jamie says, talking over a mouthful of pizza.

Ash elbows him in the ribs, narrowing her eyes at him in that silent way she has of chastising any of us when we don't act appropriately. You'd think after nearly twenty years as our manager that she'd be used to us by now.

"East is a jack of all trades," I say, feeling a surge of pride in my chest as I think of both my sons. "He's a talented guitarist and drummer. He loves drama, and he has a natural affinity for the stage, and he's gifted at sports too."

"Yet he's so down to earth about it all." Audrey smiles and her pride in her godson is obvious.

"E is definitely more laid-back," Viv says. "He feels things as deeply as Bodhi, but he doesn't dwell on them in the same way. Bodhi is more intense but also more focused. He already knows he wants to pursue a career in the music industry."

"As a songwriter," I elaborate after swallowing another bite of pizza. "He has zero desire to be up on a stage."

"That doesn't surprise me." Alex cuts into his chicken parmigiana. "He has always hated attention."

"I think it's great the two boys are so close despite how different they are," Ash says.

"It's the main reason I'm not rocking in a corner this week," Viv explains. "As long as Bodhi has E to talk to, I feel like he'll come through this."

"Are we still coming to your place for Halloween?" Jamie asks before biting a large piece of pizza.

"Of course. It's tradition." I lift my bottle of beer to my lips, taking a quick sip. "Fleur and Melody would throw a hissy fit if we didn't have our annual Halloween party. It's all they've been talking about since Oisin's birthday last week."

"Emily too," Audrey says in reference to her eldest daughter.

"We were putting Oisin to bed after his party, and he was already talking about Halloween," Ash supplies

"Oh, to be a kid again." Alex shakes his head, grinning. "When the only thing you worried about was when the next party was."

"Or what costume to wear at Halloween," Viv says.

Alex chuckles. "I remember giving Reeve such shit about that. He was always such a pussy about Halloween."

"It was the theatrical side of him," Viv says, a faraway look appearing in her eye as it often does when she talks about her first husband and my twin. "He would start planning our costumes in the summer," she adds, turning to face me.

She squeezes my thigh though I don't need the reassurance. I am confident in our love and no longer threatened by my dead brother. In fact, I like when Viv, Audrey, and Alex reminisce over the past. I like learning new things about Reeve because I never got the chance to know him in person. Something I will regret until the day I draw my last breath.

"That's actually how my passion for sewing started. Reeve always wanted us to dress in matching themed costumes, and he wanted to be unique, choosing costumes no one else would show up in."

"When we were in middle school, they would throw these lavish Halloween parties and award prizes for best costume," Audrey explains, eyeballing me across the table.

"Reeve and Viv either won or were runner-up every year," Alex says.

"Reeve was very competitive." Viv kisses my cheek. "I would be up for hours in the weeks before the party putting the finishing touches on our costumes." She runs her fingers through the scruff on my chin and cheeks. "Maybe I can make our costumes this year," she muses.

"That's a sweet thought, Hollywood, but I think you've got enough on your plate making the kids' costumes, managing the foundation, and running the household." I am trying to lift the strain from my wife's shoulders, not add to it. I do my best to lighten the load, but our label has grown a lot in the past few years, and we are still putting out albums, so I don't have a lot of spare time. We hired a nanny when the kids were younger, and we have a housekeeper and a couple of drivers to help ferry the kids to and from school, playdates, and extracurricular activities, but life is still hectic most all of the time.

I make a mental note to talk to Lauren and Jon on the weekend and see if they would be down to mind the kids so I can whisk Viv away for a naughty weekend or even a night at a hotel. She has been working too damn hard lately, and now we are dealing with all this trouble with Bodhi and the shit at school. I'm worried about her, and I want to do what I can to alleviate her stress. A night away by ourselves might be just what the doctor ordered.

Viv sighs, looking like she is carrying the weight of the world on her shoulders. "I wish I could clone myself," she jokes.

"If you discover the magic formula, please share it." Audrey finishes her pasta dish and pushes the plate away. "The clinic is full to capacity every day, and I am maxed out to the hilt."

Alex rubs his wife's shoulders while dotting kisses in her hair. "I wish I could do more."

"You gave up your career after the twins were born, and you mind the kids and run the house. You do more than your fair share." Audrey pecks his lips.

"I thought you were going to recruit a couple of doctors to come and work with you," Ash inquires, spearing the last ravioli and popping it in her mouth.

"I am trying, but the pickings are slim. There is a shortage of qualified doctors, and any I have interviewed would not be a good fit. I need people I can gel with and doctors who have the right kind of people skills. I have met so many who had an awful bedside manner. I have worked my butt off to cultivate a certain vibe in my practice, and I don't want to sacrifice that as I grow."

"What about hiring an agency to recruit on your behalf?" Viv suggests.

"I have a contact who knows one of the directors of Recruit Plus," Ash says. "I am pretty sure they have a medical division. I could put in a call and ask Sheena if you like?"

"It can't do any harm," Audrey agrees. "That would be great. Thanks, Ash."

"Aisling Fleming to the rescue again." I waggle my brows and grin at my sister.

"Is there anyone you don't know?" Viv smiles at my sister as she finishes her food and lifts her wineglass. "I can't think of a single time I have gone to you for help where you didn't know someone you could call."

Ash shrugs, letting the praise roll off her back. "Networking is the name of the game when you manage this lot." She jabs her fork in the air, pointing it at me and Jamie. "And I like to pay it forward. You never know when a contact might come in handy."

Isn't that the truth. Ash has gotten us out of more scrapes and holes over the years, thanks to her smart thinking. "We are lucky to have you. I have no doubt Collateral Damage wouldn't be the success it is without you, and the same goes for the label. We owe a lot to you, Ash."

"Hear, hear." Jamie plants a loud kiss on her lips. "You're the real rock star, babe."

"Aw." Viv clings to my arm, smiling broadly as tears glisten in her eyes. "You guys are so sweet, and Ash deserves all the praise."

"Amen, sister." Audrey lifts her glass, clinking it against Ash's and then Viv's wineglass.

My cell vibrates in my pocket, and I pull it out, frowning when I see who it is.

"Who is it?" Viv asks, tension threading through her tone when she spots my expression.

"It's East." I swipe my finger across the screen, and loud noise accosts my eardrums as I lift the cell to my ear.

"Dad!" East hollers to be heard over the din in the background. "You need to come home."

"What's going on?" I ask, sliding out of the booth and standing.

"It's Bodhi. He's lost his shit, and he won't listen to me."

"We're on our way," I say, pinning Viv with a troubled look as she grabs her purse and scoots out of the booth.

Chapter Two
Vivien

"Oh my God," I say, surveying the wreckage in front of me with disbelieving eyes. Bodhi's room is trashed. The bed is overturned, the mattress strewn across the floor, and every book and item from his shelves is scattered across the wooden floor. The globe my parents gave him for Christmas is smashed to pieces, and the autographed song lyrics Dillon had framed for him, that hung over his bed, is tossed on the floor, the glass cracked and broken. All his drawers are open, the contents upended on the floor, and a line of clothing extends from his walk-in closet to the bedroom, many of them shredded and slashed and unwearable.

None of it matters. Material things can be replaced. All I am concerned about right now is my son and the state of mind he must be in to do something so uncharacteristic. "Where is Bodhi?" I ask E, rubbing a hand along the tightness spreading across my chest.

"Your son is outside," Bobby says, and I spin around on my heel to face the man who was a lifeline for me and Easton in the months after Reeve died.

We have a team of bodyguards on payroll now, but it is Bobby and Leon I gravitate to all the time. I trust those men with my life and my family's lives, and I go out of my way to ensure they are well taken care of so they never leave.

"Leon went after him," he adds.

"I'll go find him," Dillon says, bundling me into his arms.

He holds me close, and his brief strong embrace fills me with much-needed strength. Dillon has been my rock this past week as I struggle to help our eldest son cope with the latest revelations about the past.

"Try not to worry," Dillon says even though he knows it's an impossibility. He kisses me, before letting me go. "Stay here. I will try to calm him down. Talk to East." He levels our son with a knowing look, and I can read the silent communication: Look after your mom.

Dillon leaves with Bobby, and I trail my gaze over the messed-up room as I knot and unknot my hands. Anxiety waits in the wings, ready to swoop in and toy with my insides. "Did your sisters wake?" I ask, worried at what they might have heard tonight. I bend down and start picking up debris off the floor.

Easton shakes his head, drawing a hand through his hair. "No. I made sure to close their doors and I closed Bodhi's too when he started throwing shit around the place."

I glance at him as I move around the room, gathering up the remnants of Bodhi's room. I'm on edge, and I need to do something with my hands to keep myself distracted.

Wordlessly, E starts helping, righting Bodhi's bed and flipping the mattress over, replacing it on top. He is strong from football and weight training, and it's hard to believe he's only sixteen when he's so tall and broad and looks like a grown man.

He looks so much like his father. Like Reeve too. Sometimes, I do a double take watching Bodhi and Easton together because they remind me of Reeve at sixteen, and it's like looking at a ghost. E wears his hair very similar to Reeve in a classic all-American style while Bodhi favors a more edgy look. Presently, he is wearing his hair in a faux hawk with bleach-blond tips.

"Is this a delayed reaction to what happened at school?" I ask after a while, reaching down to retrieve the broken frames from the floor.

E strides toward me. "Careful, Mom. That could cut you."

"Why don't you let me do that?" Charlotte says, entering the room, carrying a dustpan and brush and the cordless vacuum.

My inclination is to keep cleaning, but I also want to find Bodhi and Dillon. I need to see my son with my own eyes to know he's okay. "Thank you, Charlotte. Only clean up the broken things. Sweep anything that might harm him, but leave the rest. Bodhi must take responsibility for his actions. It will be up to him to fix his room."

Charlotte nods, her expression conveying her agreement.

"Thanks, Lotty." Easton gives our housekeeper a quick hug, and her eyes meet mine over my son's tall, broad shoulders. Her face shines with love. She adores all the kids, and she's so good with them, but there is a special place in her heart for Easton, and it's definitely mutual. Charlotte has been with us since E was a little baby. She never married, and she has lived with us for years, helping me to take care of our expanding family. It's safe to say we all cherish her and have happily adopted her as one of our own.

We leave Charlotte to the mess and step out into the hall-way, heading in the direction of downstairs.

E slings his arm around my shoulders as we walk the hallway on the ground level, moving toward our casual living room. "It's going to be okay, Mom." He gives me a reassuring squeeze, but I detect the uncertainty in his usual confident tone, and that troubles me enormously. "Bodhi is just going through a rough patch, but he'll pull through."

"I want to believe that," I say, striding into the room. "But this is not like him." Bodhi has always been reticent about speaking his mind, preferring to vent his thoughts and feelings onto the page than speak to me or Dillon about them. I know he has confided in Easton, and that has helped to reassure me, but lately it's as if Bodhi has pressed some inner self-destruct button, and whatever coping tools he's used in the past don't appear to be working now. I even suspect he is being more guarded with his brother, and that worries me greatly.

It's one of the main reasons why I'm so concerned.

"What happened?" I ask, turning around to face my son.

Easton wets his lips, dragging a hand through his brown hair. It's threaded with natural blond highlights, just like Reeve's hair was, from the California sun. "Don't get mad, but we watched the movie."

Shock races through me as my jaw slackens. "You did what?" I splutter as shock instantly gives way to anger. "We agreed if either of you wanted to watch it, we'd watch it together!" Pain spears me through my heart at the thought of how they both must be feeling.

Shortly after the movie premiered, some kids at school started talking shit to Bodhi and Easton about Reeve and Saffron. We went to the school immediately and handled it, but it forced us to revisit the topic of them watching it. They were only eleven at the time, and we felt that was too young to see it, but how could we protect them from other kids? That any parent would let an eleven-year-old watch an adult movie was shocking but not a surprise. A lot of parents suck at parenting.

Dillon and I had decided to let them watch it when they were thirteen. We felt that was old enough for them to be able to grasp the basics of our messy past, and we chose to stick to our guns. Yet when thirteen rolled around, the boys didn't want to watch it, and we didn't force the agenda. We told them when they decided they were ready to see it, we would watch it with them.

It wasn't optional.

It was a rule.

I know the emotional tsunami that movie will unleash in both my boys, which is why I'm livid they watched it without saying a word and without letting us be there to discuss it with them.

"I'm sorry, Mom. It wasn't planned. It was spontaneous, and you were out with Dad. I know you've been freaking out over the school thing, and I didn't want to worry you."

I sense there is more to it than this, but E is loyal to Bodhi to a fault, and I can't ever find it in me to criticize him for it. Easton has looked out for Bodhi from the minute he came into our lives, and I know he will always have his back. I love how close they are. I love how much they support one another, and I hope this movie won't do anything to damage their relationship because that would kill me.

"I didn't want you to learn the truth like that." Tears prick my eyes as I close the gap between us. I take his hands in mine. "Are *you* okay?"

A shuddering sigh leaves his chest. "Honestly, Mom, I'm pissed."

I nod, understanding why that would be the case.

"How could Reeve do that to you? How could he be so fucking stupid?"

A look of disgust crosses his face, and I hate seeing it there. But I won't criticize my son for reacting naturally to the truth or tell him he is wrong to feel the things he is feeling. "He was young and naïve, and he made mistakes."

"You told him she was a gold-digging slut! You warned him, and he refused to listen! I had him on this pedestal all my life, but he didn't deserve it."

"Don't let what you've discovered erase the happy memories you have of him, Easton. You loved Reeve, and he loved you. Every interaction between you was born of love. It doesn't excuse his actions, but he had a difficult childhood, and he felt abandoned his whole life. That made him vulnerable, but it doesn't mean he was a bad person. He was a good man who made some poor life decisions, and those decisions hurt the people he loved."

E shucks out of my hold and paces the room. "I don't know how you can defend him. I don't know how you could have taken him back after what he did to you."

"I loved him, and I forgave him. He was a good husband and a good father."

A bitter laugh rings out behind me, and I freeze as I turn around. My eyes meet Dillon's over Bodhi's shoulders. "He was a piece of shit, and my mother was a whore." Bodhi sways on his feet, slurring his words, and I'm appalled and concerned in equal measure.

"You were drinking?" I move toward my troubled son with my heart jackhammering behind my rib cage. I'm not naïve. I was a teenager once too, and things are even more advanced nowadays. Kids rarely remain kids, and they grow up way too fast. Since the boys started attending parties a year ago, we have suspected they might be drinking.

We have talked to them extensively about alcohol and drugs and encouraged them to make the right choices. Neither of our sons have given us reason to actively worry about it.

Until now.

Bodhi is obnoxiously drunk and only remaining upright because Dillon is propping him up.

"Anyone would after watching that fucking movie." Bodhi pins me with tortured blue eyes. "Why did you do that? Why the fuck did you make that movie?" Dillon grabs him when he lurches forward, stopping him from toppling to the ground. "That shit should have stayed buried with both my parents. No good comes from knowing that. I would rather you lied to me."

Pain eviscerates me from the inside out, and I'm struggling to hold on to my emotions. But I do. Because this isn't about me and my feelings. This is about my sons. They are both hurting, and it's our job to support them.

"We won't ever lie to you," Dillon says, hauling Bodhi back against his chest. "Your mother wrote that book, and we made that movie, to set the record straight. As much as all of us might want to bury the truth, it's impossible when we are celebrities and this all played out against the backdrop of Hollywood."

"We didn't want you learning about the past from the internet because so much of what was said was wrong," I say, stepping closer to him. "We didn't want you learning this without us there either. You should not have watched it without your father and me."

"It doesn't change the facts," he slurs. "I've been passed around like a sack of worthless shit. You only took me in because you had no choice."

"No, Bodhi." Tears leak from my eyes as he attempts to push Dillon away, but he's too inebriated, and Dillon is strong. "That is not the truth."

"I don't care," he shouts, struggling in Dillon's arms. "Get off me!"

"Bro." East steps up alongside me. "Don't do this. They're only trying to help. We all are."

Another bitter laugh tumbles from Bodhi's chest. "I don't need or want your fucking help!" he yells, fixing his brother with a hostile look. "I don't fucking care! It's all bullshit! No one wants me, but I don't care. I don't need anyone. People only let you down." Dillon stumbles as Bodhi continues to struggle in his hold. "My whole life has been one big fat lie."

"That's not true." Easton shakes his head. "I'm your brother. We're your family. That's not a lie."

"You're not my brother," Bodhi snarls, looking like a stranger as he fixes Easton with an ugly look. "You're my cousin." He jabs his finger in my direction. "Like she's not my mom and Dillon's my uncle, not my dad."

He pierces me with bloodshot eyes, and his face contains a world of pain I wish I could wipe away.

It's not like any of that is a secret.

Bodhi has always known who we are to him, but learning the full truth of the past has clearly twisted things and warped his way of thinking. I know it's hurt speaking. The alcohol sloshing through his veins doesn't help either. I try to remember all of this as he lashes out.

"I don't know how you can even bear to look at me after what my mother did to you. Or how you could take that piece-of-shit sperm donor back after he cheated on you with her. What is wrong with you? Why would you do that? Have you no self-respect?"

He might as well have driven a stake straight through my heart. Pain has a vise-grip around my internal organs, squeezing and squeezing until it feels like I can't breathe. I swipe at the hot tears coursing down my face as I observe the angry expression on my eldest son's face. His pain cuts me deep, and right now, I hate myself. Why did I think making a movie was a good idea? Why did I think this would help? All I have done is hurt both my boys and potentially damaged our relationships forever.

I couldn't hate myself any more than I do in this moment.

"That's enough, Bodhi." Dillon's sharp tone cuts through

the tension in the air. "You will not speak to your mother like that. She loves you, and I know you love her. I know this is hurt speaking, but I won't stand by and let you talk to Vivien like that."

With more strength than I figured he could muster, Bodhi rams his elbow back into Dillon's stomach, catching him off guard. Dillon loosens his hold on our son, and he wrangles himself free.

"You are one to talk!" Spit flies from Bodhi's mouth as he whirls around, pointing his finger in Dillon's face. "You're almost as bad as Reeve. You purposely set out to deceive her, and then you showed up and stressed her out when she was pregnant." I can't see the look on his face from this angle, but I don't need to see it to know it's ugly.

East wraps his arms around me, and I don't realize I'm shaking all over until he holds me and I feel myself trembling against him. Unshed tears fill Easton's eyes as he stares at his brother, looking utterly lost, just like he did in the aftermath of losing Reeve and Lainey. I rest my head against his shoulder and circle my arms around him, holding him as tight as he's holding me.

"I am not proud of the things I did," Dillon says. "I will regret my actions for the rest of my life, but I love your mother. I love you, your brother, and your sisters. This isn't the time to discuss it. It's late, and we all need to sleep, but I don't want you going to bed thinking you don't mean the world to us, Bodhi, because you do."

"You are our son in every meaning of the word," I add, silently beseeching him to turn around. "I hate that you're hurting. I hate that we're the reason you're in pain." Easton lets me go, and I walk up behind Bodhi, wanting to envelop him in my arms but terrified to do anything else to set him off. Dillon pulls me in front of him, wrapping protective arms around my waist as I stare up at Bodhi. "I know you are confused, but we love you, Bodhi. Whatever you are thinking about how we came to adopt you, know we did it because we wanted you to be a part of our family, and from the minute I met you, I loved you with my whole heart."

Tension is heavy in the air as he stares at me, a myriad of emotions flitting across his handsome face. "I think you're the one who is confused, Vivien."

My heart thuds painfully against my chest wall at his use of my first name. I prayed for months for him to call me Mom, and it was one of the happiest days of my life when he did. If I have lost that now, I will be inconsolable. Though it's nothing less than I deserve. I rue the day I ever made that damn movie. Bodhi already lost one mother, and I don't want him to feel like he's lost me too because that will never happen. As long as there is blood flowing through my veins and air in my lungs, I will be his mother. Easton, Fleur, and Melody's too.

"It is *guilt*, pure and simple." He hisses the word, and I flinch. "Why the hell else would you take Saffron's bastard in?"

"You can't say that to Mom!" Easton cries. "Why the hell would you say that?"

"Don't, Bodhi. Please," I whisper, trembling against Dillon.

"Don't do this, son," Dillon says. "Go sleep it off, and we'll talk in the morning."

"I don't know why you think anything will change," he slurs, knocking into Dillon as he brushes past him. "It's all a stinking pile of lies, and I'm done with it."

Chapter Three
Dillon

Vivien holds it together long enough to say goodnight to Easton, offering reassuring words that most likely sound hollow to her ears. The second East's bedroom door is closed, I scoop my wife into my arms and race down the hallway, past Bodhi's closed door and the girls' bedrooms, heading toward the stairs at the end that leads to our master suite on the next level. Vivien snakes her arms around my neck, burying her face in my shoulder as she clings to me. Her body shakes as she cries silent tears, and my heart is aching for her. For Bodhi too. Though I'm furious at him as well for the things he said to her.

Vivien is already predisposed to blame herself for this.

The last thing she needs is Bodhi cranking the guilt-o-meter to the max.

A sob erupts from Vivien's mouth when I reach our bedroom door. I hold her tight as I fumble with the door handle, eventually opening it. She bursts into loud, anguished tears as I carry her into the room, slamming the door shut with my foot. The dam breaks, and my wife falls apart in my arms as

I stride toward our bed. I sit down and scoot up to the head-board, leaning back against it as I cradle my heartbroken wife in my lap.

Vivien is full-on blubbering, and every agonized cry that tumbles from her mouth tears another strip off my heart. I hug her close, dotting kisses into her hair as she fists my shirt and presses her body flush to me, clinging to me with a desperation that equally hurts and soothes.

I love that my wife turns to me in times of need, but I hate that we are here at all.

I don't offer platitudes or fake reassurances as she cries. I won't lie to her like that. The truth is, we are at the start of a harrowing journey with no specific destination and no end in sight, so I won't tell her everything is going to be okay when we don't know if it is.

My shirt is soaked by the time Viv stops crying. Tipping her face up, she peers at me with red-rimmed, bloodshot eyes and the most forlorn expression. "I have failed him, Dillon," she croaks over an errant sob. "I should never have made that damn movie. What the hell was I thinking?"

"Sweetheart, don't beat yourself up over this. I know you're upset, but you aren't at fault here. We made that movie for the right reasons, and they still count." I brush my lips against hers, hating to see her in so much pain. "You have not failed him. You have loved Bodhi with your full heart and given him a happy, secure family life." I push damp, matted strands of her long brown hair back off her face. "We knew it would come to this. We knew the truth would be hard for the boys. But it's better than them discovering a warped version of reality via the internet. We'll support them as they come to terms with it. We'll answer their questions honestly and continue to shower them with love."

"What if it's not enough?" Her gorgeous hazel eyes widen with fear and pain as she slants me with a pleading look.

I wish I had a magic wand to solve this, but it will have to be done the hard way. "It might not be, but there is only so much we can do, Viv," I softly say, swiping the dampness from her cheeks with my thumbs. "Bodhi is drowning in self-loathing and a multitude of other negative emotions. He is going to lash out at us because we're the easy targets. He is going to resist any offer of help we suggest. He won't see what is right in front of his eyes. He won't want to accept the truth that the past really doesn't fucking matter. He won't be able to see it like it is, Viv, because he's in too much pain and he's too young to process it."

I clasp her face in my hands, peering deep into her eyes, which look more green than brown today. "Or maybe he is more mature than I was at his age. Maybe he'll see through the bullshit quicker than I did. Maybe he'll cling to us more, knowing he's so fucking lucky he has us and it doesn't matter who his bio parents are when he's surrounded by people who love him like we do." I shrug though my body is wound up tight, and I'm every bit as concerned as my wife. "We don't really know how he will react, and we must prepare ourselves for anything and everything."

"You had a family who loved you, but it didn't matter. You refused to accept it at face value. You didn't even tell them when Simon approached you and offered you money in exchange for your silence. You kept it all bottled up inside for years, Dillon. *Years*." More tears leak out of her eyes. "What if Bodhi does the same? He is like you in so many ways."

"He's also not like me in a lot of other ways. He's his own person, and we can't know how he'll react based on my circumstances and how I dealt with things."

"You've got to admit there are a lot of similarities." She winds her fingers through my hair, and I feel her touch everywhere. It helps to ground me, like always. "Maybe he'll listen to you," she continues, hope glimmering in her eyes. "If you explain how you felt and the things you wish you'd done differently, maybe you can get through to him."

"You know I will try." I tilt her face up, running my thumb along her lower lip. "I will do everything in my power to get through to him, but you have to face the fact he might not listen to any of us. He might completely break. All we may be able to do is continuously reassure him of our love and be there to pick up the pieces."

"God, Dillon. Don't say that!"

She cries, and I hug her closer again. "This isn't going to be easy, Viv. You need to prepare yourself for it. There is Easton to consider too. This won't be easy on him either."

"No." She sniffles, sitting back and lifting her head. "There is much for him to process too, and I know him. He'll downplay his own feelings because his brother will be dealing with so much more. He won't want to add to our worries, but we can't let him bottle his feelings up either. He has a right to his anger and his grief too. We need to ensure we look after both boys and that we protect the girls from any fallout." A hint of determination glints in her eyes.

There's my girl. There's my fighter. The woman who would burn the world down to protect those she loves. Viv is going to need all her inner strength to get through the difficult times ahead. And I will be there, right by her side, battling to protect our family and safeguard everything we have built over the years.

Lifting her arm, I bring her wrist to my lips and press a tender kiss to her sensitive flesh. "We are in this together, Vivien Grace. We have an amazing family, and we won't let this derail us. We will come out swinging and fighting to hold on to what we have built, and that is a rock-solid fucking guaranteed promise."

"Oh, Dillon." She repositions herself on my lap, circling her arms around my shoulders as she smiles softly at me. "I love you so much. I couldn't do this life thing without you."

"Ditto, Hollywood." I tweak her nose. "There is no one else I would want to navigate life with than you." My hands land on her hips, and I give them a gentle squeeze. "We are facing some tough times ahead, but we'll survive. We will get Easton and Bodhi through this."

"We won't ever give up on them." Steely determination underscores her tone, like I knew it would when she got over her initial pain.

"It's going to get really rough, Viv. He is going to say horrible things to us. I know, because I did. You need to remember he doesn't mean it. You need to remember you're the best fucking mother and you have given your all to these kids. Remember how much trust Reeve placed in you. He always wanted you raising Bodhi, and I know he's looking down with pride when he sees what a great job you've done. This is no measure of you or Bodhi or any of us. It's a necessary process to deal with the shit hand we were dealt by others. But we will get through this." I tuck a piece of her hair behind one ear. "What doesn't kill us will make us stronger."

She presses her lips against mine in a brief soft kiss. "I love you, Dillon. So fucking much. You are my rock. My world. My desire to keep fighting when things get tough is because you have given me the strength to be the best version of myself."

"I love you too, Vivien." I hold her face in my hands. "You have given me everything just by breathing, and I won't ever stop fighting for our family because I love our life and I will move mountains to ensure we never lose it."

She stares at me with blatant adoration and the potent need

that always lingers at the back of her eyes. "Make love to me, Dil. I need to feel our connection now more than ever."

Gripping her hips harder, I dart in and peck her lips. "You never have to beg, Hollywood. You know that. I'm as insatiable for you as I always have been."

Our sex life has suffered over the years with kids and work and the crazy chaos that is our lives, but we always make time for one another, no matter how stressed or tired we are. We may not have the time to fuck nonstop like we used to or engage in the kinky sex of our youth, but we still have regular sex, and it's always out of this world. I am so hot for my wife, and every time just gets better and better.

Viv climbs off my lap and stands, moving her hand around to the zip on her dress.

"Let me." Lust deepens my voice as I crawl off the bed. Standing directly behind her, I run my hands over her gorgeous body through her dress, loving how easily my hands fit to her curves, like they were made to perfectly slot against her. Brushing her long hair to one side, I plant a slew of feather-soft drugging kisses along her neck as I slowly lower the zip down her back. "You are so beautiful. You still take my breath away."

"Mmm." She moans softly and angles her head to the side, granting me more access to her neck as she presses back against my growing erection.

I slide the dress off her shoulders, letting it pool on the floor at her feet, while my hands wander over the silky smoothness of her tan skin. Unclasping her bra with a flick of my fingers, I drag the straps down her arms before tossing it away. I look down at her from behind as my hands reach up to cup her heavy tits. I fondle them with urgent hands, tweaking her nipples with my fingers as I grind my hard cock against her lower back and suction my lips to her neck.

Twisting her head around, I claim her lips in a passionate

kiss as one hand glides down her body and under the band of her silk panties. Two digits push smoothly inside her wet heat, and she bucks against my hand as I fuck her with my fingers. "Always soaked for me," I murmur against her lips as I roughly grab one tit while pumping my fingers in and out of her pussy. Rotating my hips, I rock against her from behind, rewarded when she moans into my mouth. I slip my tongue between her lips and worship her mouth as I angle my hand so I can fuck her faster with my fingers while my thumb rubs circles against her clit.

It doesn't take me long to work her into a frenzy, and then she's crying and calling out my name as she grinds on my hand when an orgasm rips through her. I band my arm around her waist as she milks her climax, holding her up when her limbs turn floppy, and she sags against me. My cock is leaking precum behind my boxers, and I'm dying to drive inside her and fill her to the hilt.

Lifting her up, I gently place her on the bed with her head on the pillows. I drag her wet panties down her legs and toss them aside before standing at the end of the bed, staring at the gorgeousness that is my wife.

My wife.

My woman.

My soul mate.

My goddamned reason for living.

"Spread your legs, Hollywood, and show me my pretty pink pussy," I demand as I start unbuttoning my shirt. I take my time undressing as she widens her legs, her chest heaving and cheeks flushed as she stares at me. "Lift your knees up to your chest. I want to see all of you."

She bites down on her lower lip, and I growl as I fling my shirt aside before moving to my jeans. I pop the button and rub my aching cock through the denim as I drink her in. Both holes are visible from this angle, and I would love nothing more than to fill each one tonight. But that's not what she needs. My wife needs a loving touch tonight, and I plan to deliver. "Touch your tits," I tell her as I shove my jeans and boxers down my legs, freeing my straining cock.

I strip out of my jeans, boxers, socks, and shoes, stroking my dick as I watch my wife fondle her tits while exposing her pussy and her ass to me. I am salivating and straining with the need to come as I climb up between her legs, but my needs can wait.

I want my wife to be thoroughly fucked and sated so she sleeps without trouble tonight.

Our problems can wait until tomorrow.

Right now, there is only me and Viv and our matching need for one another.

Everything else can take a hike.

Sliding on my stomach, I press my face to her delectable pussy and feast on it with my fingers and my mouth. Using her slickness, I coat my fingers and tease her puckered hole as I drive my tongue inside her cunt with relentless determination. I silently fist pump the air when she comes all over my face a few minutes later, her back arching off the bed, her nipples hard enough to cut glass, and her hips bucking, as she writhes and moans for me.

I waste no more time because I'm all out of patience and I need to be inside my woman. I push inside her in one long deep thrust, both of us groaning with mutual pleasure when I fill her up. I lean down and press a tender kiss to her lips. "I love you."

Her arms wind around my shoulders. "I love you, Dillon. You anchor me in all the right ways."

"I never want you to forget how much you mean to me. How much I worship and adore you," I say as I slowly pull out before shoving back inside her. Her legs wrap around my waist as I move in and out of her.

"I could never forget. Not when you show me in so many ways," she rasps over a moan as her tight, hot walls hug my throbbing cock.

Those are the last words we speak for a while. Both of us get lost in our lovemaking, relishing the caresses and kisses as I slide in and out of her, taking my time, bringing her to the edge and back, over and over, until we come before collapsing in a tangled heap of sweaty limbs, sated and exhausted, and bolstered by the knowledge we are a true team in every sense of the word.

As I spoon her from behind, grateful for the soft murmurings of contentment that slip from her plush lips as she drifts into sleep, I know as long as we stick together, we will weather the approaching storm and come out on the other side of it.

Chapter Four
Easton

"Babe, what's wrong?" Hollis asks, a frown marring her pretty face as she tugs at my sleeve.

"Nothing," I lie, not wanting to tell my girlfriend how bad things are between me and my brother at this point. I close my locker on autopilot as I stare at my brother down the hallway.

"Is it Bodhi?" she asks, sliding her arms around my waist as she follows my troubled gaze. "What's he doing hanging around with those guys? I didn't know he was friends with Otis and Mahlik."

"He's not." Easing her arms off me, I bend down and peck her lips. "I'm gonna catch up to him. Go to class. You don't want to be late."

She grabs the sleeve of my uniform jacket, halting my forward trajectory. "You don't want to be late either. Bodhi has gotten you into enough trouble lately."

Hollis's parents found out about Four recent suspension, and to say they weren't happy is an understatement. Her family comes from old money, and they live by old-world values and traditions. They are super strict with her. She isn't allowed out on school nights, and they impose a curfew on weekends. I might respect that if it didn't limit our time together and the opportunities to hookup and if her dad wasn't a giant asshole.

He looks down his nose at my parents because of their celebrity status and how they made their money. I couldn't give two shits what Mr. Astor thinks really, except it matters to my girlfriend, and I'm crazy about her. We got together at the end of summer break, and we have been pretty much inseparable since then.

Best two months of my life.

"Stop worrying." I kiss her again, hating I can't linger. "I'll see you at lunch."

She palms my cheek and smiles sadly at me before turning around and walking in the direction of her first class. I sprint down the hallway, calling out to Bodhi as he starts walking off. He ignores me, and I clench my fists at my sides as familiar annoyance bubbles to the surface.

I am so sick of this bullshit.

I wish to fuck we'd never watched that damn movie.

"Wait up!" Grabbing a fistful of his shirt, I yank Bodhi back. Otis and Mahlik slow their pace, turning to look. "I need a word with my brother—*in private*," I say, hoping they get the hint.

They don't. Leaning against the wall of lockers, they stab me with hostile looks that might scare some people, but not me.

"Fuck off." Bodhi wrestles out of my grip and turns to glare at me.

"You can't keep ignoring me forever." I eyeball my brother, pretending like the two assholes aren't listening to every word.

"I don't want to talk to you." Bodhi purposely shoves me, and I can't get over how much he has changed in such a short span of time. Unless he was hiding this part of his personality for years, stewing over the past, and now it's all come rushing to the surface, like a dormant volcano sprung to life.

Bo works out with Dad in our home gym, and he's bulked up a lot this past year, but he's still not a match for my strength, and I don't so much as flinch when he shoves me. Coach puts us through our paces every morning before school and most evenings at practice, and my body is a solid block of muscle. "I'm your brother, and this shit isn't cool. I'm not the enemy, Bo." I lower my voice as I lean in closer to him. "Why are you shutting me out? We need to talk about this. Turning on one another is not the way to handle it."

Bo has always been quiet and introspective. Except with me. We always tell each other shit, and it hurts that he's pushing me away and refusing to speak to me. This past week has been a total shit show. Mom is crying all the time but trying to hide it. Dad is attempting to break through Bo's walls and get him to open up, but he's getting nowhere. My little sisters have picked up on the tension, and they're acting out. "You're not the only one hurting. It's hurt me too."

He snorts out a laugh and levels me with a look that can only be described as hateful. "Of course, you would make this about you." He shoves me again, and I'm starting to get angry now. "You are so fucking selfish and so self-centered. What the fuck do you have to be angry about? You're not the one who was dumped on and abandoned his entire life. But poor E. The attention is on me this time, and you don't know how to handle it, so you try to make it about you. Fucking typical."

Otis and Mahlik laugh, and my hands clench at my sides. I want to knock their two ignorant heads together and unleash some of the burning frustration racing through my veins. I am literally speechless. I cannot form a single word in response to the utter bullshit that has just streamed from my brother's mouth.

I grind my teeth to the molars as I stare at the stranger in front of me. This is not my brother. I don't know who Bodhi is anymore, and he's really starting to scare me.

We need to have this out but not here.

"We'll talk at home."

"Are you deaf?!" Bodhi moves to shove me again, but I step back.

If he pushes me one more time, I will not be responsible for my actions, and I really don't want to fight my brother.

"I want nothing to do with you," he hisses. "Leave me the fuck alone."

Pain spreads across my chest as I watch him walk away, and I hope it's not prophetic.

"Okay, spill," Hollis says from our table tucked into the corner of the cafeteria. "What is going on with you?" Usually, we eat at the jocks' table with my teammates, their girls, and some of the cheerleaders. But I'm not in the mood for company today. Hollis didn't protest, readily letting me drag her to the quietest spot in the place so I can lick my wounds in relative obscurity.

I shrug, wanting to talk to her but not wanting to broadcast my family problems to anyone outside the house either. "Just some shit at home," I say before stuffing the last of my sandwich into my mouth.

"I am a good listener if you want to unburden." She pierces me with a concerned look as she slides her arm around my shoulders and presses into my side.

Her gorgeous big blue eyes radiate sincerity as she stares at me, and I loosen the hold on my tongue, deciding I need to talk to someone about it before I explode. "Bodhi and I watched the movie about our parents last week. Now, he's pissed and taking it out on all of us. He won't talk to me at all, and I'm worried about him."

Her eyes pop wide. "You only watched the movie now?"

I nod. "My parents asked us if we wanted to watch it the day after my thirteenth birthday. I wanted to see it, but Bo was adamant he didn't want to know. It was an all-or-nothing situation, so we told our parents no."

"Let me guess, all that shit at school started this." She rubs her hand up and down my back, and her touch is comforting.

"Yeah. It flipped a switch in Bo, and he was moody and withdrawn all that week we were suspended. My parents were out at dinner when I discovered him watching it in his room. I freaked because we'd promised we would watch it together with my parents, but Bo refused to turn it off, so I watched it with him, and then all the shit hit the fan."

"I'm sorry, Easton. I can't imagine how much that must have hurt."

"Have you seen it?"

Slowly, she nods. "I don't say this to make you feel bad, but I reckon most kids at school have probably watched it. Your mom is the daughter of Lauren Mills, and she's totally stunning. Reeve was a famous movie star, your dad is a rock legend, and they're both seriously hot."

I shove her arm away and glare at her. "That's my fucking dad, Hollis. You can't say shit like that about him."

She holds up her hands in surrender. "I take it back. I didn't mean anything by it, just trying to explain why people have a vested interest in watching the movie. You and Bodhi are two of the most popular guys at school. I could name countless girls who would kill to be in my shoes, and Bodhi has that moody, broody, bad boy vibe going for him that has tons of girls lusting over him. You two are a big deal around here, and your family history only adds to the appeal. My mom said it was quite the scandal when it was revealed your mom was in love with twins and that you were actually Dillon's son and not Reeve's."

"Jesus, Holl. Could you say it any louder?" My head whips around, but thankfully no one is paying us any attention.

"No one is listening," she says, deliberately lowering her tone this time. "I felt sad for your mom watching the movie. You could tell she really loved Reeve, and I was crying when Saffron broke them up. But then she met Dillon, and oh wow." She rubs a hand across her chest as a dreamy expression appears on her face. "He was amazing, and you could tell they had this epic kind of love, and then when she went back to L.A. and Reeve was waiting for her, I couldn't help but think how lucky she was to have found that kind of love twice."

I think my girlfriend might be a little bit insane or delusional, or maybe it's a bit of both. "I don't think my mom's intention was to romanticize everything she went through. Both my dads put her through hell, and we will be dealing with the fallout of all their shit for the rest of our lives. There is nothing amazing about that."

She purses her lips, looking like she's ready to argue with me, but I'm done. "It almost sounds like you're in love with my dad. Are you using me to get to him?" I half joke because I'm getting a weird vibe off her now. Or maybe it's just me because I'm having a shitty day and I haven't slept properly in weeks.

"Don't be ridiculous. I'd have to be invited to your house to use you to get close to your dad, and you still haven't asked me to meet your parents."

I stare at her like she's grown an extra head. "Are you for real right now?"

She shrugs, looking at me like maybe I'm the crazy one, and I give up. I don't have the mental capacity to deal with this shit at the moment. I bury my head in my hands. It's that or strangle my girlfriend. I know she's only trying to help, but she's making it worse with every word that comes out of her mouth.

"I'm sorry, East," she whispers, linking her fingers through mine under the table. "I suck at this. I don't know the right thing to say, and I don't want to hurt you. Of course, I'm not in love with your dad. I'm in love with *you*. So completely and utterly totally in love with you."

I curl my fingers around hers and lift my head, kissing her softly, as her words melt my frustration. "I love you too." I nuzzle my nose against hers. "I know you mean well, babe, and it's cool. Don't mind me. I'm just extra sensitive right now."

"I get that, and I understand. I am here for you, and I have an idea." Her eyes spark to life as she tosses her long blonde hair over one shoulder and leans in, pressing her warm mouth to my ear. "I know how to relax you. I can hang around after cheer practice and wait for you. I'll tell my mom I'm studying at the library. Meet me under the bleachers in our spot, and I'll make it up to you."

"I love you," I whisper, lifting Hollis to her feet and planting a hard kiss on her mouth. I can taste myself on her lips as I kiss her while tucking my cock back in my boxers and pulling my zipper up.

"I love you too," she rasps in a breathless tone as I back her up against the wall in our spot under the bleachers.

"I needed that," I say as my fingers creep under the short skirt of her cheer uniform.

Her fingers wind around my wrist, stalling my upward trajectory. "You don't have to do that. I like looking after you."

I dart down, pressing my lips to that sensitive spot under her ear. "As I like looking after you. My dad would kick my ass if he knew I let you blow me first. He told me to always look after my girl's needs before my own."

"Your dad seriously gave you sex advice?" Her face contorts into a funny expression, like she can't decide if she likes it or is disgusted by it.

I chuckle as I caress her outer thigh. "You said it yourself. My dad is a rock legend, and he's blunt as fuck. He doesn't hold back, and he always tells it to me straight. My mom was with my dad when they gave us the sex talk at ten, but she doesn't know Dad spoke to me and Bo again when we were fourteen. He gave us condoms and the safe sex speech but also spoke to us about respecting women, ensuring it was fully consensual, and to make sure we treat them right."

"I guess I have your dad to thank for your magic fingers then," she purrs, letting my wrist go.

"Don't start that shit again," I growl, only half joking. "The only person you can thank for my magic fingers is me," I say as I push her panties aside and slide the magic inside her slick warmth.

"Call me later," Hollis says, leaning through the window of her BMW to press one final kiss to my lips. "And don't forget we are picking up our costumes tomorrow after school." Her best friend is throwing a Halloween party at her place, and most everyone from school is going. I am looking forward to it. I need to release some of this pent-up frustration, and losing myself in my girl and a gallon of beer sounds like the perfect solution.

"Drive safe," I say, blowing her a kiss. I watch her drive out of the mostly empty school parking lot before I walk toward my SUV.

I decide to stop at our local bakery on the way home to pick up some treats for Mom and my sisters. It's a French bakery, and Mom adores their almond croissants and lemon tart meringue. I pick up some of them along with a box of macaroons for Fleur and Melody, an éclair for Dad, and cinnamon apple pies for Bo and me.

I know what Bodhi said earlier, but I'm not giving up on him. He's my brother. We're as close as twins. Hell, most of the kids at school think we are twins because we look so alike. I know that was only anger speaking earlier. Maybe the pie will soften him up and he'll agree to at least sit down and talk to me. Despite what he said, I don't give a shit about me. Bo is the one who was crapped on by Reeve, and I need him to know I am here for him. That I get it and he can vent to me. A part of me understands why he might not want to talk to me about it, but that's exactly why he should.

We aren't responsible for the things Reeve did.

It doesn't change who I am to Bo or who he is to me.

I need him to know I always have his back and he's my brother through and through.

It doesn't matter that I can't reconcile my memories of the man I called Daddy Reeve with the knowledge I have of him now.

I swallow over the messy ball of emotion as I unlock my car and set the cake boxes down on the passenger seat.

It's a cluster fuck of epic proportions, and I still can't process how I feel about the fact Reeve chose Mom and me over Bodhi. It's wrong on so many levels. My heart aches for my brother as I start the engine and glide out into traffic. I have only gone a few blocks when I spot my brother's truck, parked at the curb, outside a bar that is a known hangout for bikers and career criminals.

An ominous sense of dread tiptoes down my spine as I park my SUV and get out to investigate. It's almost sunset, and the darkening clouds casts gloomy shadows on the pavement as I walk toward the bar. A noise from the alley to the left of the bar claims my attention, lifting all the fine hairs on the back of my neck. Cautiously, I pop my head into the alley, crouching down as I spot three indistinct figures up ahead. Keeping low and tucked in tight to the wall, I creep up the alley, stopping a few feet from the men and hiding behind a smelly dumpster.

Panic sluices through my veins when my brother's voice rings out loud and clear. "Thanks, man."

There's a rustling sound before a man with a deep unfamiliar voice says, "Nice doing business with you, dude."

I flatten my back to the wall at the sound of approaching footsteps, hoping I blend into the shadows, as a figure walks by. Bodhi's expression is grim, his body rigid with stress as he strides past me without noticing.

My heart slams against my rib cage as I watch him shove the packet of pills in his back pocket and exit the alley.

Chapter Five
Bodhi

I thrust into the busty blonde from behind, rubbing her clit as I drive into her one final time before spilling my load in the condom and roaring my release. The brunette underneath her moans and writhes on the bed as the blondie licks her pussy. I'm guessing it's still slippery from my dick because I fucked the brunette first before moving on to her friend.

I'm high as a kite, a mix of narcotics and alcohol sloshing through my veins, but at least I remembered to wrap my dick before I took these two girls up to one of the bedrooms in Otis's house. At least that is one good thing Dillon taught me. I shudder at the thought of ever knocking a girl up. That is something that will never happen.

I'm never having kids.

My DNA is way too fucked up to consider bringing more mini-Reeves or mini-Saffrons into the world.

My blood boils, like it does anytime I think about Reeve or Saffron or Mom or Dillon. To think I used to look up to my dad.

Want to be like him. Hung off Dillon's every word like he was some kind of god.

What a fucking joke, I think as I pull out of blondie and flop down beside her on my back. I grab my joint where I left it on the bedside table, light it up, and take a toke, inhaling deeply as my mind wanders over the shit show that is my so-called life.

Adults suck.

Every single adult in my life has either screwed me over or let me down. Dillon included.

He's as selfish as the rest of them. If he hadn't been such a cunt the night Vivien left Ireland, my entire life could have been completely different. If he had claimed his woman, Vivien never would have returned to Reeve. Maybe Reeve wouldn't have abandoned me then. I don't harbor any delusions he would have been with Saffron. That whore was one seriously crazy bitch. He clearly regretted letting her mess with his life in such a destructive way. He never would have gotten with her if she permanently ruined things for him with his childhood sweetheart.

Saffron Roberts was a lying, cheating, stealing, whoring, good-for-nothing, gold-digging slut, and I hope she is rotting in the fiery pits of hell. It is nothing less than she deserves. That bitch didn't give a shit about me. I was a means to an end for her. When her blackmail backfired, she was willing to terminate her pregnancy without giving her baby, *me*, a second thought. Then she took drugs while pregnant, uncaring how that might impact the baby growing inside her.

She truly was a selfish bitch.

"Babe." The brunette slinks over to me, pressing her nonexistent tits to my side and pinning me with fake doe eyes. "I need your cock again."

I shake my head and swat her hand away when she reaches for my dick.

"Ah, come on," the blonde says, getting in on the act again. She crawls between my legs, pushing them apart. "It's not every day we get to screw a rock legend's son. We need to make the most of it."

I explode, venting all my aggression in the wrong direction. "Get the fuck away from me, you slut." I shove her shoulder with my foot, pushing her back, and swing my legs around, planting my feet on the edge of the bed. Looking over my shoulder, I glare at both of them. "You're both whores and lousy lays. All women are gold-digging sluts with ulterior motives." I jab my finger in their direction. "You have just proven that fact." Blondie scowls, opening her mouth to retaliate, no doubt. "Shut your skanky mouth, and get the fuck out."

"Fuck you, asshole," she says, climbing to her feet.

"I told you we should've held out for the other twin," the brunette says, flipping me the bird as she scrambles to her feet, hurriedly pulling her slutty dress back on.

Her words roll over me like water off a duck's back, but I know they might register and hurt when I'm sober. "My brother wouldn't touch either of you even if you paid him," I say, turning around on the bed and sitting up against the headrest.

"Doesn't say much about you, does it?" Blondie retorts, squeezing her massive tits into a bra that looks way too small to contain them before shimmying into a tight black dress.

"No underwear. How classy," I snarl, pulling my boxers and jeans on. Reaching down, I swipe my T-shirt off the floor and yank it over my head.

"Loser," Blondie says, glowering at me as she yanks the door open, and the two girls storm out into the hallway.

"Good riddance," I mumble as I stand, thrusting my hand out to hold on to the wall when my body sways and the room spins.

"Holy shit," Otis says, appearing in the doorway a few seconds later. "What the hell did you say to the girls? I have never seen Nellie so angry. Mahlik will kick your ass if you hurt his sister."

"Which one is his sister?" I ask, not realizing one of the girls was related to my new friend.

There is a hierarchy at the snobby private school I attend with my brother. The token scholarship kids stick together and don't usually mix with the rich kids. Not sure where I fit in the scheme of things. Or life, in general, anymore. I only hung around with the popular kids because of my brother. But they are his friends, not mine. It's time to change things up, and the truth is, I feel more at ease around Otis, Mahlik, and their crew than I do my so-called own kind.

Mahlik lives in a foster home and Otis lives in this rundown two-story three-bed two-bath house in a less than desirable part of LA. Mom would throw a hissy fit if she knew I was here, but she thinks I'm tucked up in bed, licking my wounds and nursing my sore feelings.

Well, fuck that shit.

I'm done wallowing. Done letting the sins of the past impact me.

I'm singing my own song now, and if my parents and East don't like it, tough shit.

Otis and Mahlik are good people, and they keep it real.

"The brunette," Otis says, halting the rambling thoughts in my head.

"She has no tits," I blurt, shoving my feet into my boots and trying to ignore the way my eyes can't focus. "And they were both shitty lays."

Otis barks out a laugh. "You are way more talkative when you're trashed, man." He slams his hand down on my back. "We should definitely do this again."

"For sure."

Somehow, I stumble out of the house and manage to call an Uber to take me home.

<hr>

I have lost all sense of time, but I don't care. My head is buzzing, my body is tripping, and I feel alive. Grabbing a bottle of JD from the liquor cabinet in the living room, I wander out to the garden, casting a quick glance at my cell phone as I stumble across the grounds at the back of our house. I have a shit ton of missed calls and messages from my brother. A pang of longing slaps me in the face before I wrangle that shit back into a lockbox where it belongs.

Easton is not my brother or my friend or even my cousin.

He is nothing. He can be nothing to me.

He is the physical representation of everything I will never be, and I can't stomach looking at him.

Opening the whiskey with my teeth, I swallow a large mouthful, welcoming the burn as it glides down my throat. I keep drinking as I head in the direction of the memorial garden, growing more and more angry as my thoughts churn and rage reignites in my veins.

"You're an asshole," I roar when I reach the garden with the tree replanted from our old house and the bench Dillon lovingly carved from wood. Two plaques are nailed to the bark. One with Reeve's and Lainey's names on it and the second one is in remembrance of Lori. My first mother. "You're both assholes," I amend, leveling a glare at Lori's name. "You lied to me until you were forced into telling me the truth," I snarl, tipping my head back and shouting at the stars, hoping wherever she is Lori is hearing this. "You let this happen. You were too soft on Saffron. You let her get away with too much, and then you passed me off to Vivien like a sack of old clothes when you could no longer care for me. You left me too!"

My head whips around, and I narrow my eyes as I glare at Reeve's name. I advance toward the tree, trampling the flowers underfoot. "But you." I jab my finger into the wood, wishing I'd had the forethought to bring a screwdriver with me so I could chisel through his name and erase it in the way I wish I could erase it from my brain. I try to pry the plaque from the bark, but it's nailed in tight, and it doesn't budge, no matter how hard I tug at it. "You were a pathetic, weak prick who cheated on the woman he professed to love and abandoned his baby son. Why?!" I roar before knocking back more whiskey. "How could you give me away? I was just an innocent baby."

A sob rips from my throat, but I shut that shit down. None of them deserves my tears. Only derision. I bark out a laugh as I glance down at the colorful flower beds, remembering how East and I helped Vivien to plant this memorial garden after we moved into our new house. Fleur was young, but she helped too. What a joke. To think I used to find solace coming out here and talking to my dad and Lori. Now I know neither of them deserved it.

Fueled with a fresh layer of rage, I let out a roar as I flip the bench and drop to my knees. I dig up the flowers with my nails, ripping out roses and shrubs and other colorful flowers, mashing them between my hands until they are completely destroyed, growing more enraged with every passing second as I remember how I used to draw comfort from coming out here and talking to them. I hate how fucking gullible I was.

But no more. My eyes are fully open now.

"Stop!"

My head jerks up at the sound of my brother's voice. Easton is jogging across the grass in sleep shorts with his feet shoved into untied sneakers. His fist is closed around something in his hand, and the expression on his face is a mix of pity and anger. I sit back on my butt and lift my knees, bringing the bottle of JD to my lips as I survey the carnage around me with a satisfied grin.

"What the fuck is wrong with you?" East yells, and I feel a sense of pride I got him to raise his voice. He's always so fucking happy and amicable and far too laid-back. It's good to see him rattled.

"What the fuck is wrong with *me*?" I snap, champing at the bit for this fight that's been brewing for days. I clamber awkwardly to my feet, still struggling to focus, and it's an effort to remain upright.

"Look at the state of you, bro. You're totally wasted." He dangles my bag of goodies from his fingers. "How could you do this? This will kill Mom. You know what she went through with Reeve, and Saffron was a known junkie." He takes a step toward me, pain comingling with concern on his face. "This isn't the way to deal with things. This is a one-way trip to hell, and I'm not going to stand by and watch you throw your life away."

I laugh. He still doesn't get it. "You don't get a say."

"The hell I don't. I'm your brother. You might have forgotten what that means, but I haven't."

"I hate you," I roar, throwing the bottle of JD at his head. He ducks down, and it soars over him, landing somewhere in the grass behind him.

"You don't."

"I do." I march toward him, putting my face all up in his. "I hate you. If you didn't exist, if Vivien didn't exist, he wouldn't have abandoned me."

East sucks in a sharp gasp. "You don't mean that. Take it back."

"No." I shove his shoulders, understanding I am in no fit

state to fight my brother but uncaring. I need to hit something, and his smug face will do. I swing my arm around, but he easily blocks me, wrapping his hand around my fist and staring at me in shock.

"What the fuck, Bo? Stop this."

With my free hand, I punch him in the stomach, but it lacks power because my limbs aren't cooperating and I can't pack any strength behind it. "I am sick of you always coming first," I hiss.

"C'mon, bro. That is not true, and you know it. Mom and Dad have always treated us equally."

I swing for him again, glancing the side of his jaw with my fist before he pushes me away. "Stop trying to fight me."

"He chose *you*!" I yell, wrapping an arm around my middle as intense pain jumps up and slaps me from within. "He gave me up without any hesitation because he loved you and he loved Vivien. I was nothing to him!" I roar, not even aware tears are rolling down my face until salty moisture trickles over my lips. "It's a miracle he didn't agree to let Saffron abort me. He would have done the world a favor if he did."

"No, Bo. No." East lunges toward me, and I seize the opportunity, thrusting my fist in his face and landing a decent blow to his nose. East stumbles back, losing his footing as he trips on one of his laces, tumbling to the ground.

I jump on top of him, pummeling him with my fists. "I hate you. I hate he picked you. I hate I will always be second best. That I'm never good enough for anyone." I lash out with my words and my fists, and East just takes it. "Fight me, you coward!" I land a particularly vicious punch to his temple, and his eyes darken as murderous rage finally sweeps over his features.

Features I hate are so similar to mine.

Then it's on.

We roll around the garden, punching, kicking, and grappling with one another, and it's the most alive I have felt in weeks. Pain rattles around my skull and spreads across my stomach as East enters the spirt of things, but I don't care, continuing to throw punches and shout insults at my brother.

"What the fuck are you doing?" Dad says, appearing out of nowhere and grabbing me off Easton.

I thrash about in his arms, continuing to expel insults and expletives as I watch Vivien help East to his feet. My brother is clutching his side as Mom inspects his swollen nose and the bruise mushrooming on his cheek. I'd say I fared the same, if not worse, but I don't care. It felt good to do that.

"This has got to stop," Mom says, imploring me with her tone and the pleading expression on her face. "Please, Bodhi. Please stop this."

"He was fighting me too!" I yell, struggling to get out of the vise-grip Dad has me in. "But, of course, you take his side! Everyone is always on his side."

"That is not true, and you know it," Dad says.

"Bullshit! I always come last! Reeve sacrificed me so he could have Vivien and Easton. He didn't give a shit what happened to me. Abandoning their baby was so easy for him and Saffron."

"We need to talk about this—properly talk about this," Mom says, walking closer to me. "There is so much you don't know. Things you need to let us tell you."

Tears stream down her face, and for a second, I hate I'm the one who put them there. But it quickly passes; incinerated by the raging anger that burns continuously through my veins. "I know you took me in out of pity and guilt. Did it make you feel less foolish, Vivien? Was it your way of proving you were better than them? Take in the poor orphan and appease the knowledge you were the reason my father gave me away. Raise me with the golden boy and pretend like you weren't the catalyst for all of this."

"That's enough," Dad snaps, tightening his hold around my body, but I'm only hitting my stride now.

"You were such a dumb bitch, Vivien. You let both of them play you, and you continuously forgave them. You're as weak as Reeve."

East pulls his mom into a hug, tugging her back as he glares at me with something akin to loathing.

Good.

At least the feeling is mutual now.

"This isn't you," she says, hastily swiping at the tears coursing down her face. "This is anger and whatever drugs you pumped into your body because I see your eyes rolling in your head. I know you're on something, and it's okay. It will be okay."

I laugh because she is so fucking delusional. "I'm just living up to my birthright. Reeve threw you under the bus for a high, and so will I. I might not look like her, but Saffron's blood flows through my veins. I was always destined to be a junkie. Nothing was ever going to save me from this fate."

"No one believes that bullshit," Dad says, turning me around and grabbing me by the upper arms. "Least of all you. You are your own person, Bodhi. You are not the sum of the people who gave you life."

"You're such a fucking hypocrite!" I yell. My stomach churns, and nausea crawls up my throat. "You turned to sex, drugs, and booze when you discovered the truth, or did I misinterpret that part of the movie?"

"Don't make the same mistakes I did. You are smarter and more focused than I was at your age."

"I'm worthless," I admit, all the fight leaving me as nausea washes over me in heady waves. "No one wants me. Everyone is destined to leave me or push me away. You guys took me in out of pity. You don't really care for me. I'm a way to assuage your guilt. Nothing more. So just leave it alone. Nothing any of you can say will ever make me believe otherwise."

My gaze bounces between them, and I feel numb inside, which is weird because I'm a giant mass of pain. Every cell in my body is drowning under the torrent of anguish obliterating me from the inside out.

I want it to stop.

All of it.

"You know I'm right, so let me accelerate this next part of the process," I say before I jerk to the side and puke my guts up all over the ruined memorial garden.

Chapter Six
Vivien

"That's the last of the trash," Audrey says, entering the kitchen with Ash in tow. They are carrying black sacks filled to the brim with dirty paper plates and plastic silverware from the kids' party. In addition to our gang, we had twenty boys and girls from Fleur's and Melody's classes this year, and it was absolute mayhem. The guys are supervising the trunk-or-treat taking place in our driveway, and then it will be time for all the outsiders to leave. I can't say I'm sorry. It has been hard to enter into the spirit of Halloween this year with the way things are with Bodhi.

It's hard to function, period, right now.

I am not sleeping well, and my appetite is virtually nonexistent. I am so worried about Bodhi and worried about Easton because he's pushing his own feelings aside to try to be there for his brother, and I know he doesn't want to add to our stress. That only compounds the guilt and the fear. The only saving grace is the girls seem oblivious. Bodhi is acting normal with them, and I'm grateful for that small mercy.

My children are the only reason I get out of the bed each morning, and I won't stop trying for them.

My husband is the other reason.

Dillon is my rock, holding me and loving me every night as we confide our fears in one another. I crawl into bed a wreck each night, collapsing in his arms, and we lose ourselves in one another, needing kisses and touches to remind us of who we are and the things we have overcome already. Then we sit and talk for hours, and every night, my husband papers over the cracks in my heart, reminding me I'm not in this alone.

We haven't even spoken much to anyone outside the family. One, I don't want to worry them either. And two, I think it's hard for anyone to relate unless you are living with this. Dillon and I are even closer now. A feat I never thought possible because we're as close as a couple can be, but in a weird way, this situation is strengthening our bond on an even deeper level. I love how he is the strength I need to get through this, but he's also not afraid to be vulnerable with me, sharing his fears and concerns and letting me bolster him in the same way he's doing for me.

It's how I know we will survive this. We will get our boys through this. Love has to be enough. And we won't ever stop fighting for our family.

I have never been more in love or more in awe of my husband.

"Are you getting work done in the garden?" Ash asks, interrupting my inner monologue. She squints in the direction of the memorial garden as she peers through the window.

Dillon laid a temporary fence around the area until we have time to repair the damage Bodhi wreaked on the space. "Bodhi destroyed the memorial garden a couple nights ago when he was trashed," I calmly explain as I open the refrigerator and grab a fresh bottle of white wine. "Dillon and I had to pull him and East off one another in the middle of the night. They were throwing punches and wrestling on the ground like they weren't as close as twins."

"Shit." Ash dumps her garbage bag at the door to the laundry room and walks toward me with concern shining in her eyes. "That's a bloody nightmare, and so unlike my nephews. I take it things aren't any better on that score?"

I shake my head, swallowing over the thick, painful lump in my throat, as Audrey removes three clean wineglasses from the overhead cupboard. "Things are terrible, and Bodhi won't speak to any of us. It's like I don't even know my own son anymore. It's like a stranger is wearing his skin. My sweet, intense, deep thinker has disappeared, replaced with a boy who is so angry he has forgotten how much he is loved." A strangled sound rips from my mouth, and my lower lip wobbles as I struggle to contain my emotions.

"Ah, Viv. Don't cry, babe." Ash drapes her arms around me as Audrey pours the wine, pinning me with sympathetic eyes.

Audrey knows more than most because we sought out her advice. We needed her knowledge of mental health and the law to understand our options. That was a depressing conversation for sure.

"I saw him outside with the girls a few minutes ago," Audrey says, handing me a glass of wine. "Melody was on his shoulders, and he was holding Fleur's hand as they went from car to car, so all isn't lost." She hands a wineglass to Ash when she eases out of our embrace. "That sweet boy is still in there. You can still get through to him. Try not to lose all hope."

We take our glasses and head to the living room to wait for the guys. Dillon has some surprise lined up, and he told us to wait here until we were called. I really am not in the mood this year, but Dillon insisted we party it up like usual, and I'm glad he was so pushy. It's important to keep things normal for the girls, and a night of wine and catching up with my girlfriends is just what I need.

"Did you talk to that therapist I recommended?" Audrey asks when we are settled on the comfy couch.

I'm wearing the Sandy costume I made—a tight off-the-shoulder black top, matching black leggings, a belt with a gold and black center clasp, and open-toed red sandals with a high heel—while Audrey and Ash are dressed as Frenchie and Betty from *Grease*. I curled my hair and temporarily dyed it blonde with one of those wash-out color spray cans, to really look the part.

Dillon is wearing a tight black T-shirt, black pants, and boots—it didn't take much for him to transform himself into a white-blond version of Danny Zuko. Jamie is dressed as Kenickie, and Alex is Doody. It's the first year all three couples have coordinated outfits, and I have a sneaky suspicion this is all tied into my husband's surprise.

Did I mention how much I love him and what a lucky bitch I am to call him my man?

Audrey peers at me expectantly, and I try to focus my wandering mind. "Yes. Dillon and I met with her yesterday. Bodhi is still refusing to see her, but she is going to come over one night next week and see if he'll talk to her then." She also recommended a therapist for Dillon and me to speak to, and we have an appointment arranged for next week. We need all the help and support we can get because we're floundering, so I'm willing to try just about anything if I think it will work.

"Good luck with that plan," Ash says, kicking off her heels and pulling her feet up onto the couch. "I remember how much of a nightmare Dil was when he went off the rails. My parents tried everything to help him, but it was like talking to a brick wall." Her brow puckers, and her nose scrunches up. "Actually, it was worse than that. A wall doesn't have an attitude and lie to your face."

"We can't sit by and do nothing. He's doing drugs, and he's drunk every night. He's full of self-hatred, and I'm so worried about him."

Ash sits up straighter, leveling me with a troubled stare. "You don't think he plans to hurt himself, do you?"

"He's already hurting himself, Ash, and yes, I'm worried about suicide." I set my glass down and bury my head in my hands, drawing deep breaths as I try not to descend into a full-on anxiety attack. I can scarcely swallow over the messy ball of emotion clogging my throat, and I'm clinging to my sanity by my fingernails.

Audrey runs a soothing hand up and down my back.

"Can you force him into rehab or therapy?" Ash asks. "If you are genuinely worried he might try to kill himself, are there legal measures you can adopt?"

"You'd think there would be," Audrey says in a clipped tone as I lift my head and try to compose myself. "California law states minors over twelve can be forced into rehab; however, if a professional determines the child is mature enough to participate in the decision, they often defer to the kid. Most kids don't want to go to rehab, so they say they didn't mean it and they're not addicted. There is a seventy-two-hour emergency hold for a minor if they are gravely disabled, like when there is an acute medical event. I have seen cases where kids have OD'd several times, some were even clinically dead for a short period, and the courts still refused to sanction the hold order or let the parents sign them into rehab. I understand why some of these measures were put in place, but the whole system is wrong. Parents' hands are really tied in these situations."

It's not anything Audrey hasn't told us already. She was the first person we called the morning after the garden incident. What she explained left us feeling so impotent. Powerless to do anything to help our son. At least if there was something we could do, it would feel like we were trying and maybe making some progress. But there is little we can do except sit and watch this unfold—however it's going to unfold—and it's killing me slowly.

I feel like I'm dying inside.

My kids are my world, and to know one of them is suffering and in so much pain and I can do nothing to stop it or help him is unbearable. Easton is hurting too, but he's trying to put a brave face on, and I hate that for him. His feelings matter too, and I'm trying to be there for both my boys, yet I feel like I'm failing them.

There is no rulebook or parental guidebook for dealing with this. Winging it is not in my nature, but we have little choice. We are ambling around in the dark, blind and terrorized, unsure if we're going the right way or heading toward a black hole we won't be able to crawl back out of.

"I could try talking to him," Ash offers. "You know my past. I tried to kill myself, and I regretted it almost instantly. Maybe my experience might help."

"I don't know, Ash." I swirl the wine in my glass. "It might just put more ideas in his head." I knock back a mouthful of wine. "Or maybe it would help. Maybe he might open up to someone outside our immediate family." I shrug because I have never felt more helpless or more clueless. "It's hard to know what the best thing to do is. We are walking on eggshells around him. Dillon has tried to break down his walls. Out of all of us, he can relate the most to what Bodhi is going through. But Bodhi is angry with Dil too, and he just doesn't want to hear it. He won't even go into the studio if his dad is there."

"Mom."

We jerk our chins up at the same time, the three of us looking over at Easton standing in the doorway.

"Hey, love." I force a smile on my face, hating that smiling no longer comes naturally.

"Can I talk to you for a minute?"

"Absolutely." I set my wineglass down and stand.

Chapter Seven
Vivien

"You stay," Ash says. "We'll go see what the guys are up to."

Easton shakes his head. "Dad said if you even attempt to peek he's locking you in the laundry room for the rest of the night so you'll miss out on all the fun."

"Your father is going to get a swift kick in the arse when I see him," Ash replies.

"Let them do their thing," Audrey says, topping off Ash's wineglass. "It's not often we get time to ourselves without the kids or the guys. I say we make the most of it."

"I won't keep Mom long," Easton says as I walk toward him.

"Enjoy your party," Audrey says, waving at him.

"Don't do anything I wouldn't do!" Ash calls out.

"I have a license to do whatever I want, so..." East quips, waggling his brows at his auntie.

Ash barks out a laugh. "That's my nephew!"

I appreciate they keep it light and neither of them references the large purple bruise on East's cheek or his swollen nose. Thankfully, it wasn't broken, and though both of them walked away with bruises and cuts, no one suffered serious injury. For that, I'm grateful. "I hope that costume comes with a mask," I say when I step out into the hallway, tugging on the black cape flowing over my son's broad shoulders.

East closes the door behind me. "It does, but it's creepy as fuck, and I didn't want to scare the little kids." He lifts a shoulder. "Can you walk me to my car? I'm already late, and Hollis is a stickler for punctuality."

I'm not sure I like the sound of his latest girlfriend. All of her family are snobs, and she sounds a little too controlling for my like. She has lasted longer than most of them, and I get the sense he's more serious about Hollis than any girl that has come before. And there have been a lot. E is a serial dater, and there seems to be no shortage of girls willing to go out with him.

Bodhi is the complete opposite. He hasn't had a girlfriend, at least not to our knowledge, though I am sure there are girls or maybe guys. He's too handsome not to garner interest. We are very open about sexuality, but neither of our sons have come outright and said they are hetero or otherwise, and we would never ask. They are entitled to their privacy, and if there's something we need to know, I'm sure they will tell us in time.

"What is Hollis dressing as?" I ask, keeping step beside my son, which is no easy feat with his long-legged strides. East is as tall as Dillon now, and if he keeps growing, he will end up taller, something he loves teasing his dad about.

"She's an angel to my devil." He grins, waggling his brows as he grabs a scary demonic red mask with horns and a tall black pitchfork from inside the hall door.

"Will your brother be at this party?" I ask, my stomach churning with anxiety at the thought of the mayhem Bodhi could indulge in on a night like tonight.

"That's what I wanted to talk to you about," East says,

looping his arm in mine. "Bo will be at the same house party. He left already, but you don't need to worry. I won't drink, and I am going to watch out for him."

I slam to a halt, peering up at my son with tears in my eyes. "You are such a good son, Easton. And a good brother, but this is not your responsibility. It's not your job to keep Bodhi in check. You have your own life to lead, and we want you to live it."

"I know, Mom, but I can't not do it. I will always have his back, especially when he's hurting so bad. I am worried about him but super pissed too. The stuff he said to you the other night is not right, and it made me so angry, but I know he doesn't mean it. Like he doesn't mean the shit he said to me. He might have abandoned me, but I won't abandon him."

I fling myself at Easton, bundling him into a tight hug. "You are so loyal and so strong." I lean back and raise my hand, palming one side of his cheek. It's still so weird to feel a hint of stubble on his face. In my mind, Easton and Bodhi are still my little boys. "You make me proud every day, East. I know this isn't who Bodhi is, and he needs us to be strong for him. But we are here for you too. I know the truth has upset you as well."

"It's worse for my brother."

"It's not a competition. You are entitled to your feelings, and they matter to me and your dad. You can talk to us about it. You have always idolized Reeve. I can only imagine what you must be thinking and feeling now."

He shrugs, and a muscle clenches in his jaw. I rub his hand, and maybe we shouldn't have started this conversation now, but I need Easton to know we are worried about him too. I know I asked him to be strong, but he has a right to be mad or upset or confused or all of those things.

The situation with Bodhi doesn't negate what Easton is going through.

"I feel guilty, Mom," he says, almost in a whisper. "Bo was right when he said Reeve gave him up for us. That was wrong on so many levels. How could he do that? Especially after the way Simon treated him and Dillon. I just don't get it."

I squeeze his hand. "Reeve isn't here to tell us for sure, but I think he knew I wouldn't have been able to take Saffron's child in at that time in my life. I think he was afraid if he kept Bodhi, he would lose us, and he feared he would come to resent him and neglect him the way Simon did to Reeve."

"He didn't even give you the chance to consider it though. You're a good person, Mom. I know you wouldn't have turned Bodhi away. Dad thinks so too."

"You spoke to your father about this?" Dillon hasn't said anything to me, which isn't like him.

"We talked briefly while we were outside with the kids."

Ah, that explains it. "I'm not sure what I would've done. I hated Saffron, and I was very confused over my feelings for Reeve and Dillon. I like to think I would have taken him in, but Lori was there. She was his flesh and blood too. I might have considered that the best option."

Easton shakes his head. "You wouldn't have, Mom. You knew Reeve inside and out. If you'd known Bodhi existed, you would have taken him in. You loved Reeve more than you hated Saffron, and I know you'd never have turned an innocent baby away."

Tears prick my eyes, and I have never felt prouder than in this moment. "I love you, E. I am so proud of the man you are becoming."

Easton envelops me in a warm hug. "I love you too, Mom. Bodhi loves you as well. He's too angry to do anything but lash out now, but I know what's in his heart. He loves you and Dad. He loves our family. We just need to remind him of that."

"We will, son." I ease back, smiling up at him, needing to

get these words out because I don't want Easton paying the price for Reeve's sins. "Reeve loved you so much, Easton. I don't ever want you to doubt that. I know it pained him to give up Bodhi. I know he never stopped thinking about him. It doesn't make it right, but I don't want you carrying misplaced guilt. Reeve always wanted a family. It had been denied to him growing up, and he'd led quite a lonely existence, outside the times he was with me and your grandparents. His greatest wish was to be a father and to have a family of his own. You gave him that. *We* gave him that. I hate what he did to Bodhi, and I don't know if I can ever forgive him for his actions, but I am glad Reeve got to experience family life with us before he died. He wasn't a bad person. He was a good person who made bad decisions, and a lot of that was because of the neglect he endured as a child. He craved love, and it often blinded him to the facts. The best way we can honor Reeve and support Bodhi is to love Bodhi with all of our hearts and to be patient and kind as he struggles to deal with the truth."

"I know, Mom. I am trying to be there for him even when he makes it hard."

I lean up and kiss his cheek. "We can't ask any more of you, Easton, and you are not shouldering this alone. You come to us anytime with anything. All we want is what is best for both our sons."

Chapter Eight
Easton

"Wow, your brother sure seems determined to party hard," Lewis says, as we stand at the corner of the room watching Bodhi knocking back beers like they're water. A posse of girls from school surrounds him, fawning over him and vying for his attention. His bruised face and the shiner he's sporting—thanks to yours truly—only seem to add to the appeal. Some girls are weird.

Otis, Mahlik, and the rest of that crew are lapping up the additional popularity Bodhi has brought to their door, looking like their shit doesn't stink. I honestly couldn't care less, except for they scene they have introduced my brother to. "I don't like it. It's not him. Bo has been strictly antidrug, and now it's like he's forgotten every single code he lived by."

"It's probably just a phase."

Lewis slaps me on the back, oblivious to the turmoil churning in my gut. Although he's my best buddy, I haven't told him what's going down at home. The only person who has a clue is Hollis, but she hasn't pried since that day in the cafeteria, and I haven't volunteered any more information. She didn't

65

need to ask me to know it was Bodhi I got in a fight with. I'm pretty sure the whole damn school knows just by looking at our faces.

"You should cut loose," he adds. "No point in both of us drinking soda. You can leave your car here tonight, and I'll pick you up tomorrow to come get it."

Lewis is on the football team with me, and he takes it very seriously, rarely partying, even after a win. I like a few beers, as much as the next guy, but I try not to overdo it. I work hard to keep in shape so I'm at the top of my game, and being healthy is important to me. I had plans to go a little crazy tonight, but that was before Bodhi and I got in a fight and beat the crap out of one another.

Now, I can't drink. Not when Bo is already smashed and showing no signs of slowing down. One of us has to remain sober. "Thanks for the offer, man, but I need to remain sober. I told Hollis's dad I'd drive her home, and I promised my mom I would watch out for my brother."

"Bodhi is lucky to have you because I gotta say it. He's asking for trouble hanging around with those dudes. I hear they're into all kinds of shit."

"I don't doubt it." I just hope Bodhi has enough sense left not to get mixed up with worse shit. However, I'm not feeling overly confident as I watch him smoke a joint while a hot redhead grinds on his lap, practically dry humping him in front of everyone.

"Let's go find the girls," I say, needing a few minutes reprieve.

We move into the next room, and I find my girl in the middle of the dance floor, shaking her tempting booty and curling her fingers in my direction. Lewis's current fuck buddy happens to be Hollis's best friend and the girl hosting the party. Chelle is dancing in the same circle as Hollis, so we join them.

"Baby, you're here at last," she slurs, flinging her arms around my neck and pressing her tits up against me. "I thought you'd ditched me."

"Never, babe." My gaze roams over her gorgeous body, both loving and hating how much skin she's showing. If it was all for me, no problem whatsoever. But the tight bra top shows way too much cleavage, and the little tutu skirt barely covers her ass. She has glittery white angel wings strapped to her back, and she went heavy on the makeup tonight. I prefer her when she wears less, but I can't deny she looks hella hot. "You look gorgeous," I whisper in her ear, swaying my hips and rocking against her.

"And you're wearing far too many clothes." She pouts, running the tip of her finger up over the red muscle top covering my chest and arms.

"You picked this, remember." I circle my arm around her slim waist.

"We could always go to the bathroom and strip you of a few layers." She waggles her brows in a flirtatious manner as she simultaneously stumbles on her feet, and I have to steady her to keep her upright. She is still slurring her words, and her eyes are a little blurry.

"How much did you have to drink, babe?" I ask, moving us in time to the beat.

"Just some wine coolers. Oh, and a few vodka shots." She flips her fingers up. "Maybe four or five." Her brow puckers as she continues flipping fingers up. She giggles. "Possibly it was more like six or seven." She shrugs, like it's no biggie.

"How the hell did you drink that much in a couple hours?"

"I have been here since four. I came over to help Chelle get everything ready."

That makes more sense. She's clearly drunk, and though I'd

love to take her upstairs and fuck her, I'm not having sex when she's not in a position to make any such decision.

She seems to have forgotten about it anyway, so we dance for a few songs, bumping and grinding against one another, kissing and making out, and I finally feel myself relaxing.

A while later, I head outside to the patio area to join my buddies. I pop my head into the main room on the way, checking to ensure Bo is okay. He has a girl draped on either side of him on the couch, and he's taking turns kissing and groping them. Bo isn't usually one for PDAs, and I have never known him to have a threesome. Sure, he's hooked up with girls, but it's always singular, and he's never shown any interest in girls other than sex.

His eyes open as if I called him, and his head lifts, our gazes locking. A new, familiar snarl curves the corners of his lips as he flips me the bird. Pain dances across my chest as I push my way through the room and head outside. The fresh air is a welcome balm to my troubled soul, and I walk in the direction of my buddies, grateful to be away from the stifling atmosphere inside.

We leave our girls dancing inside as we sit around the pool, drinking beer and shooting the shit. Talk mostly centers around our next game, which is against our biggest rival. They beat us last year, and we are determined to nail their asses to the wall this time.

"What's up with you sind Bo?" Niall asks, blowing smoke circles in the air as he passes the spliff to the guy beside him. "I thought you two were close." He gestures toward my face. "We all know you two got into it, but we don't know why. What went down?"

"It's none of your business," Lewis says, taking a quick drag of the joint. "Just drop it."

"Is it about Hollis?" Niall asks, arching a brow.

"Why the fuck would you think that?"

He kicks his legs out, crossing his feet at the ankles. "I saw them eye fucking one another in the hallway at school on Friday."

"Shut the fuck up," Lewis says. "You just love stirring shit." My best friend turns to face me. "Ignore him. He's an idiot."

"If you say so." Niall smirks at me like he knows something I don't.

His words piss me off enough that I get up five minutes later to go and check on my girlfriend. I head into the main room first, but Bodhi is nowhere to be seen. I storm over to his friends, folding my arms across my chest as I level a look at Mahlik. "Have you seen my brother?"

He looks me up and down, leaning back in his seat and crossing one leg over his knee. The redhead who was grinding on my brother's lap earlier is tracing her tongue up and down his neck, and I guess my brother's new sharing habit is a result of hanging out with these guys. I don't want to be judgmental when I don't know the guys, but I see how my brother is chang-ing, and I don't like their influence on him.

"Answer the question," I snap, all out of patience.

"I don't know where Bo is, but even if I did, I wouldn't tell you." Mahlik turns to the redhead, claiming her lips in a hard kiss as he blatantly dismisses me.

Asshole.

I exit the room and head into the next one in search of Hollis. My heart crashes around my chest as I inspect the dance floor and the rest of the room, finding no sign of my girl-friend. I gulp back bile as a feeling of dread washes over me. Rubbing the back of my neck, I take a final scan of the room, spotting Chelle on my second inspection. I stalk toward her and press my mouth to her ear. "Where is Hollis?"

She pins me with bloodshot, unfocused eyes as she giggles,

clinging to my arm. "I thought she was with you," she slurs, trying to drag me into dancing.

"Where did she go?" I ask, rapidly running out of patience.

"Try the guest bedroom," she says. "She usually stays in the pink one."

I maneuver my way out of the packed room, taking the stairs two at a time, while trying to ignore the acid crawling up my throat.

He wouldn't do this.

I know things are shit between me and Bodhi right now, but he wouldn't cross a line.

I'm not sure I could say the same about Hollis. She's drunk, and she was horny earlier, and I've been getting weird vibes off her all week.

I reach the long hallway on the second level, which I assume houses the bedrooms. I open and close doors, apologizing to the couples I interrupt. I'm down to the last two doors, one on either side of the hallway, when a familiar voice curses out loud, lifting all the hairs on the back of my neck. The sound came from the room on the left, and my hand flies to the door handle.

Without hesitation, I fling the door open and barge inside, pain tightening my chest when I find my girlfriend stark naked on the bed with her mouth gliding up and down my brother's cock.

"What the actual fuck?" I roar, clenching my hands into fists at my side.

Hollis shrieks, releasing Bo's cock from her mouth with a loud pop. Her red lipstick is smeared all over her face, and saliva pools around her mouth and dribbles down her chin.

"East," Hollis whispers, scrambling off the bed and walking toward me. "I can explain," she slurs, almost tripping over her feet.

My arm darts out to steady her before she takes a fall. I am so disappointed in her. I really liked her, and I thought she felt the same. Now, I'm wondering if she wasn't using me to get to my brother all along.

"She is drunk and not thinking clearly," I shout at my brother. "You shouldn't have come up here with her." I want to believe Hollis wouldn't have done this if she was sober, but I can't say that for sure. Bodhi knows better though. Dad drilled this into us. What's to stop her turning around and claiming he forced himself on her when she's so drunk I doubt she even remembers her own name?

"Tell yourself whatever you must to feel better, *brother*." Bo sneers as he wraps his hand around his dick, giving it a few pumps. "She's been coming on to me for weeks. Hollis was the one who came looking for me tonight. She knew exactly what she was doing."

"Baby. It's cool." Hollis runs her hand up my chest, and though my inclination is to push her away, she is completely smashed, and I won't hurt her.

She doesn't have such qualms though.

"It's true. I want him, but I want you too." She licks her lips and attempts to bat her eyelashes, and it's pathetic. Slowly, I peel her hand off me and step back. Bo is still on the bed, stroking his dick, and I'm disgusted with him and so fucking angry at both of them.

"I don't share," I snap at her. "And I don't date cheaters either."

"C'mon, babe." She makes a grab for me again, swaying on her feet, and I curse under my breath as I reach out to steady her again. "It'll be fun. I've always wanted to do twins." Her eyes light up, and I wonder what the hell I ever saw in this girl. "Don't pretend like you're shocked. It's practically your legacy."

Anger surges through my blood, and the vein in my neck pulses violently as I see red. "What the fuck did you say?" I roar. "I bet Daddy would love to hear this. He thinks his little girl is such a good girl, but I know the truth. You're a self-serving slut, and I don't know what I ever saw in you."

Bodhi barks out a laugh, but I see the rage in his eyes and the tension in his jaw. He's as pissed at her comments as me, but his stubborn need to hurt me overrides his true feelings and doing the right thing. He narrows his eyes at Hollis. "If anything goes down, it goes down on my terms." Shifting his attention to me, he shoots me a sneering look. "Reeve and Dillon shared Mom. Maybe we should see what all the fuss is about?"

My blood boils as I glare at him. "You take that back." I prod my finger in the air, working hard not to lose my shit. "You can't say shit like that."

"I can say whatever the fuck I want."

"This whole fucking nightmare started because our dads both wanted Mom!" I shout. "Don't you dare make light of this or attempt to glaze over it. Be careful what you say next, Bo, because I'm all out of patience with you."

He glares at me, and tension bleeds into the air as we stare at one another with so much emotion and so many things left unsaid filling the space between us.

If you'd asked me even a month ago if anything could ever tear me and my brother apart, I would've laughed in your face and told you to stop saying stupid shit.

I cannot believe we are here and that things have sunk to a new low. In the grand scheme of things, Hollis doesn't matter one little bit. Except for what she represents. I don't know if I can ever forgive Bo for this. If our relationship will ever recover.

I know he's hurting, but that doesn't give him a free pass to betray me.

Bo breaks our staring contest first, ignoring me as he gestures toward Hollis. "Slut, get over here and finish sucking my dick."

And he's made his choice.

Pain mixes with frustration and anger inside me, and I'm close to the edge.

This was the time to pull back on the bullshit, and he made the wrong choice.

Hollis glances between Bo and me, biting on her lower lip in an obvious tell. Drunk as she is, she's not oblivious to the clear tension between me and my brother, and it's evident she's torn over what to do.

I decide to help her out because I'm not torn over this decision. "I'll make this easy for you," I tell her. "We're done. I want nothing more to do with you."

Bodhi barks out a laugh. "This wasn't your decision, and you know it, but you just can't bear to lose face, can you, *brother?*"

He's so full of shit. Even if Hollis does want him, there's no way he actually genuinely wants her and no way in hell her parents would let her date Bodhi with his current attitude.

His eyes roll back in his head as Hollis makes her decision and climbs up on the bed. Bodhi grabs her arm and pulls her to him. She giggles, kissing his neck as he purposely gropes her, deliberately trying to hurt me. "Tell me, Easton. How does it feel to take second place to me? How does it feel knowing I have taken something that belonged to you?"

"If this is some fucked-up form of revenge, you lose. Hollis doesn't matter." I grind my teeth to the molars, struggling to hold myself in check.

Hollis *doesn't* matter, but Bodhi does.

I can't believe he is doing this.

How can a person change so much so fast?

Where the fuck has my brother gone, and do we have any chance of ever getting him back?

"Really?" He quirks a brow as he lifts her up, positioning her over his body. "Little slut, ride my cock. Show my brother how much you matter."

I should walk away. My head screams at me to do that. To be the bigger man, but I can't make my limbs move. It's like I'm frozen in place, watching in horror as my brother drives the knife in deeper.

There will be no coming back from this.

His eyes never stray from mine as she lowers her pussy down over his cock. She moans, throwing her head back and rocking on top of him as rage becomes a festering inferno in my veins. Bodhi sits up, keeping her on his lap, sucking her tits and grinning at me like a maniac as he tugs her nipple with his teeth.

"Holy shit!" someone says from the open doorway behind me. "You guys, you gotta see this."

Hollis is so out of it as she rocks up and down on my brother's dick, she doesn't realize they have gained an audience. Bo laughs as he thrusts up inside her while glaring at me like he hates me. Laughter rings out behind me, and humiliation mixes with anger and pain as the hold on my control snaps, and I lunge across the bed, wrapping my arm around my brother's neck and dragging him away from my ex-girlfriend as Hollis screams.

Chapter Nine
Dillon

"D il." Vivien shakes me, and I slowly rouse from slumber as my phone vibrates across the top of the bedside table. "Babe, wake up."

"I'm awake," I mumble, reaching my arm out for my phone as I blink my eyes open.

"That's the second time it's rang in succession." She sits beside me as I haul myself upright and lean my back against the headboard.

I stifle a yawn as I swipe my finger along the screen, not recognizing the local number. I glance at the time. No good can come from an anonymous phone call at three a.m. I brace myself for bad news as I wrap my free arm around my wife, press the cell to my ear, and answer the call.

"Dad!" Easton's panicked tone greets my eardrums.

"What's going on?" I ask while mouthing "East" at Vivien.

"Bodhi and me got arrested. We need you to come get us."

A muscle clenches in my jaw as I instinctively tuck my wife closer to my side. "Where are you?"

"We're at the Hollywood station on Wilcox Avenue."

"I'll be there as soon as I can," I say, removing my arm from around Viv and flipping the covers off.

"Thanks, Dad." His voice sounds meek in a way that is not characteristic of my son.

The call ends, and I grip the phone tight in my hand as I swing my gaze to my worried wife. This is going to kill her, but there is no way to sugarcoat it. "The boys got arrested. I need to go get them."

"What?" she splutters, her eyes popping wide. "Why?"

"I don't know the details." I pull her into my arms and hold her. She's shaking, and I hate what this is doing to her, especially at a time when the foundation is growing at an unprecedented rate and she's so fucking busy. She should be enjoying seeing her hard work come to fruition, but instead she takes no pleasure from it because she's so worried about the boys. Bodhi in particular. "Stay here." I lean down and kiss her. "Try to sleep. You have a big meeting tomorrow."

"Fuck the meeting, and fuck staying here." She climbs over my lap and off the bed. "We're in this together. I'm coming with you."

I stand and pull her into my body because I'm very needy these past few weeks. I always have to be near her. To reassure myself she's okay. To offer what little comfort I can with my touches and my kisses. If I could take on all of her pain, I would because I hate seeing her so upset. "Are you sure?"

"One hundred percent. Let's go get our sons."

"I see the word is already out," I say, over a resigned sigh, when I drive up to the entrance of the Hollywood station, spotting a handful of paparazzi hanging around outside.

"I think those guys always hover around police stations hoping to land a juicy story."

"It's widely known cops are paid to leak tips to the vultures." I maneuver our car into a free spot at the curb alongside the drab redbrick building and kill the engine. Bobby and Leon pull up behind us in one of the security SUVs.

"Either way, there's no avoiding this."

I stretch across the console and kiss her. "We'll get the PR people on it in the morning and spin the narrative the way we always do." Lifting her hands, I kiss her fingers. "Don't stress it, Viv. The media are the least of our worries."

"I don't want this to make it harder for the boys."

"There is nothing they can say they haven't already said over the years. Fuck 'em, Viv. They don't matter."

"You're right. Let's go."

We exit the car at the same time, and I run around the hood to reach my wife, clasping her hand and keeping her close as we stride toward the entrance. Bobby and Leon exit their car and come up either side of us, shielding us from touch. The bloodsuckers notice us immediately, lifting their cameras and snapping pics as we make our way inside. We ignore the questions they throw at us, keeping our gazes firmly fixed ahead. As soon as our feet hit the ramp with the star-studded overlay, they hang back and leave us alone.

Inside, we talk to an unfriendly jackass behind the desk until Carson Park, the Lancaster family lawyer, shows up and takes control. Viv had called him when we were en route. His arrival is timely as I was seconds away from punching the unhelpful asshole glaring at me like I have committed some crime.

"Take a seat, and let me handle this," Carson says, pointing over our heads at the waiting area. "Keep your head down and your mouth shut, Dillon."

I glare at the dick. "Last I checked, you're not my father and I'm a grown man who knows how to control himself. Go do your job and get my kids." Sliding my arm around Vivien's shoulders, I turn us around before I land one on his annoying face.

I still hate him, but he's a damn good lawyer, and it made sense to retain his services rather than having to move all our business to a new firm. We sold most of the assets in Simon Lancaster's portfolio to raise funds for the foundation Viv set up in the aftermath of Reeve's death, and Carson ensured that everything went through smoothly.

The Reeve Lancaster Foundation for Child Actors now boasts tons of famous donors including actors, directors, producers, movie studios, and other personnel involved in Hollywood. Along with the funds we raised, there is a decent pool of money to execute Vivien's vision for the foundation. Child advocacy consultants are the new norm on movie sets, with most of their salary being paid by the foundation.

The meeting Vivien is attending tomorrow afternoon is with the heads of most of the top studios in Hollywood to get their sign-off on the new governing rules for child actors which they have all agreed to support. It is the culmination of years of hard work to get to this point, and I am so proud of her.

She is truly making a difference.

Viv is ensuring child actors are kept safe and protected on movie sets with rules around the number of hours they can work per day. Guidelines are being implemented so that each actor is assigned a qualified tutor on set, ensuring their education doesn't fall behind. A list of restrictions on promotion and other activities that expose them to the seedier side of the industry has been drawn up. The advocacy consultant has a team of experts to call on should additional support be required, like therapists, doctors, trainers, and a whole host of medical and health specialists to ensure all their needs are being catered to while on set.

Not every studio is on board, and there is still a lot of work to do, with fundraising being an important ongoing activity. Viv, with help from Ash, has built a team of people around her to help to manage the foundation, but her personal workload in recent months has been extreme, and I can tell she is struggling to cope right now.

This is the very last thing she needs, and I am going to knock those boys' heads together when I get my hands on them.

We take seats on the hard, uncomfortable chairs in the waiting room, with Bobby and Leon flanking us, and settle down to wait.

Carson returns thirty minutes later with a surly Bodhi and a remorseful Easton in tow. Vivien rushes to hug the boys, and I want to slap sense into Bodhi when he stands there like a statue, refusing to hug his mother back. I don't know how much more of this behavior I can tolerate.

He can rant and rave at me as much as he likes, but he sure as shit is not going to disrespect his mum.

These past few weeks have made me realize, all over again, how much of a little prick I was to my parents back in the day. I even called Mum to apologize again. I didn't tell her how bad things are with Bodhi because I know she'll worry and there isn't much she can do from Ireland. She thinks it's normal teenage bullshit we're dealing with, and she even joked about karma biting me on the ass.

If only it were that simple.

"Are they being charged?" I ask Carson, in a low voice, as I watch Easton hug his mother, holding her for longer than usual to make up for his brother's failing. Commendable as it is, that boy has got to stop taking on everyone else's responsibility.

Carson shakes his head. "I wrote a check to cover the damages and secured an agreement from the Peltzes' attorney that they won't be pressing charges."

"What did they do?"

"They were at the Peltz house attending a Halloween party. Apparently, they got into a fight over a young lady, and then others joined in. It got vicious, and someone called the police. There was a lot of damage to the bedroom and the upstairs hallway." Carson leans in close, talking into my ear. "Bodhi resisted arrest and refused drug and alcohol testing. He's lucky because he is clearly on something, and he smells like a brewery. If we hadn't arrived when we did, they most likely would've gotten a warrant to take a blood and urine sample."

I doubt much would've happened if it was confirmed he's high and drunk, but he doesn't need a record or the media spinning the bullshit they would if they discovered this truth. I can just imagine the headlines now and how they'd tie his behavior to Reeve's and Saffron's addictions.

"Thank you." I mean it sincerely. Carson might be a pain in the ass to deal with, but he's a shrewd, skillful pain in the ass.

He nods. "You know I value your family business, and I apologize if I was out of line earlier. You're not always known for your restraint."

"I know, but I'm not an imbecile either. You need to give me some credit."

"Noted. You and Vivien should stop by the office soon. I'll be retiring next summer, and my son is taking over the practice. I'd like to introduce you to him and start handling the transfer."

I quirk a brow. "I thought you'd retire the day they carted your dead ass out on a stretcher."

He chuckles. "So did I." He clamps a hand on my shoulder. "But it was either that or get a divorce, and I love my wife. I think she has suffered enough. Besides, none of us are getting any younger."

Isn't that the truth.

"I will leave you to take these young men home. I trust they'll have learned a lesson."

That's highly debatable in Bodhi's case, but I don't articulate the thought.

We walk in silence outside, all of us keeping our heads down and ignoring the larger throng of paps on the sidewalk as we make our way to the car.

"I'm sorry," East says when I have pulled away from the curb.

"What happened?" Viv swivels in her seat, staring at our sons in the back seat.

I glance at Bodhi through the mirror. He's staring out the side window with a newly familiar apathetic look on his face, but he's not nearly as indifferent as he'd like us to believe. He holds himself stiffly, and a muscle throbs in his cheek as he grinds his jaw while glaring at the outside world like he's pissed at everything and everyone.

And I get it. I haven't forgotten those feelings. I just wish I knew how to get through to my son. I wish my experiences could connect us in a way where I'm in a position to support him and help him. But nothing I could say will get through to him. Tough as it is to accept, he needs to process these feelings and go through the pain in order to come out on the other side.

All we can do is let him know we love him and that we are here for him.

I return my attention to the road, casting a quick glance at my other son. East is equally as tense and ignoring his brother too. His brow puckers, and he scrunches his nose, like he always does when he's thinking. I only noticed recently how Ash does the same. Genetics are fascinating.

"Is someone going to answer me?" Vivien says, a hint of her anger and frustration breaking through.

I reach across the console and squeeze her hand. "Maybe we should wait until we get home to have this conversation."

"He fucked my girlfriend," Easton blurts, shocking both of us.

"Hollis?" Viv says, her gaze bouncing between East and Bodhi.

"She's a slut," Easton adds. "Which makes her perfect for *him*." He snarls as he glares at Bodhi.

Bodhi turns his head, smirking at his brother, and I'm tempted to stop the car and take both of them outside to beat some sense into them.

"Shrinks would have a field day with you and all your mommy issues," he adds as Vivien says, "Easton! That's enough."

Ignoring Vivien, he continues. "And that's before they get to the daddy issues. You're just like them. Selfish, an addict, and incapable of loyalty. I have done nothing but watch out for you from the moment we met."

His voice elevates a few levels, and Viv and I exchange a troubled look. I want to tell him to zip it until we get home so we can discuss it fully when I'm not driving, but East has been bottling shit up for weeks, and I don't get to dictate the timing.

If he needs to get this off his chest, I'm not going to stop him.

In a way, having this conversation in the car is perfect. It's not like they can avoid it when we're trapped within such tight confines.

Pain stabs me through the heart as I see how East is literally trembling with anger.

He jabs his finger in Bodhi's direction. "My parents took you in and treated you as an equal part of this family. All they have ever done is loved you and supported you. They have given you everything, and you don't get to treat me or them like this!" he shouts.

"Pull over," Viv says as I'm already slowing down. I pull off to the side of the road and kill the engine. We aren't far from home, but East is on the verge of a meltdown, and it can't wait.

"You're a disloyal prick, and I hate you!" Easton roars as Vivien climbs out of the passenger seat and opens the back door.

Bodhi has an impassive expression on his face, and I don't even know if his brother's words are registering.

"As long as I live, I will never forgive you for this," East says. "From now on, you're dead to me."

Chapter Ten
Vivien

"How are you holding up?" Audrey asks as I pile more pancakes on the plate on autopilot.

"I'm not," I truthfully admit. "Bodhi is even more withdrawn. It's been a week since they were arrested, and he hasn't spoken one word to Dillon or me. Easton is still mad at him, and they aren't talking. Not that I blame E. It was a huge betrayal, and he has every right to his anger. The therapist came on Tuesday, and that was a shit show."

I pour more batter into the mold on the skillet, staring into space as I recall one of the worst weeks ever.

I've endured a lot of heartbreaking things in my life, so I don't say that easily.

"East spoke with her but didn't want to talk about it with us after, which we had to respect," I explain. "He was withdrawn and quiet the rest of the night. Then Dillon frog-marched Bodhi into the living room where he sat in silence for a half hour while the therapist tried to coax him into talking to no avail."

"Jesus, Viv."

"He refuses to eat meals with us. He leaves for school early and doesn't come home until after midnight most nights. He removed the GPS tracker from his truck and his cell so we have no clue where he is or what he's up to. He's either drunk or high when he returns or sometimes both. Last night, Dillon confiscated the keys to his truck because we're terrified he's going to wrap it around a pole and kill himself or hit an innocent person."

My hands shake as I flip the pancakes over. I'm still a nervous passenger and I cross myself every time the boys leave in their cars. I think I will always worry about car accidents after what I lived through, but there is a very real possibility of it happening now with Bodhi because he has become reckless and shown he has little value in living. "I can't concentrate at work. I was a total basket case presenting at the conference last weekend though thankfully I had already done the groundwork and all the studios signed off on the new child advocacy rules."

"That's a big win, Viv. You should be so proud. I know Reeve would be."

"Gawd, don't mention his name because I'm so fucking pissed at him." I lift the pancakes out of the skillet and drop them onto the plate. "He started all of this, and I'm angry at him all over again." I glance at the clock. "Is eleven thirty too early to hit the vodka because, I swear, I want to drink myself into blissful numbness and pretend like this is all just a nightmare."

"Breathe, Viv." Audrey takes my hands and rubs them. "Let me finish brunch. Go take a bath, and we'll go for a walk then."

I shake my head and retract my hands. "I'll finish brunch. I'm trying my best to keep things normal for the girls." Emily, Fleur, and Melody attend a dance class at ten a.m. every Saturday morning, and it's tradition for them to come back here and have pancakes and strawberries.

"Who's hungry?" I say, in my loudest, cheeriest voice, as I lift the plate and head toward the large wooden kitchen table where our three princesses are currently coloring while they wait to be fed.

"Me, me, me!" they respond enthusiastically as one.

"I want the biggest pancake 'cause I'm the oldest and it's my birthday in ten days," Fleur says, licking her lips as she watches me approach.

"I want the biggest pancake 'cause I'm the youngest and I've got the most growing to do," Melody chips in.

"What about you, Emily?" I ask Alex's and Audrey's eldest daughter, who at seven is slap bang in between my two girls. "Don't you want to stake a claim?"

"Nope. I don't care what size pancake I get as long as there are lots of them." Her goofy grin is adorable, and I love that little girl as much as if she was my own.

I lean down and press a kiss to her cute blonde head. She is the sweetest child and so affable. "Don't ever change," I tell her, my voice cracking a little.

"I hate to break the news to you, girls," I tell my daughters as my gaze darts between them. "But all the pancakes are the same size because I got a new pancake mold." I set the plate down in the center of the table.

"Everyone gets the biggest!" Melody says, clapping her hands as I watch Fleur grab three pancakes and dump them on her plate. That girl has the appetite of an elephant, but she's as skinny as a rail, and I have no idea where she puts all the food she devours. Not that I'm complaining. For a kid, she's very adventurous and willing to try anything. Melody is a picky eater, and I have to sneak vegetables into sauces and blitz them until they are hidden so I can get some goodness into her. If I left it up to her, she'd live on a diet of chicken nuggets and grilled cheese sandwiches.

"Can I have a chocolate cupcake after my pancakes?" Fleur asks in between bites as I place a few strawberries on all their plates while Audrey sets a glass of freshly squeezed orange juice down in front of the three girls.

"You can have a cupcake later. You don't want to make yourself sick."

"I love chocolate cupcakes," Emily says before popping a piece of pancake into her mouth.

"My brothers loooooove chocolate cupcakes," Melody says over a mouthful of pancake. "But Mom hasn't made them in ages."

It's true. The foundation has kept me super busy, especially this past year, but recent weeks were a lesson in prioritizing what's important. I'm interviewing for an operations director at the moment—Ash is helping with it—and once I have someone in the role, I plan to take some time off to focus on my family. Going forward, I aim to work only while the kids are at school. I want to have more time to devote to my family. That has always been my goal, but lately it's been hard to stick to it. The foundation needed more of my time, but now it will have to take a back seat.

My kids and my husband take precedence.

I haven't been able to sleep properly for weeks, so I have been getting up early and baking. I find it therapeutic. The boys loved chocolate cupcakes when they were younger, and it's silly, but I thought it might help to remind Bodhi of his youth and help him to remember all the fun times we had as a family. I leave a bag for him and Easton at the door every morning with a homemade smoothie and a cupcake in each one. Both bags are gone every day, but I don't know if Bodhi is taking his and dumping it in the trash or if E is taking both so as not to hurt my feelings.

"Your mommy is very busy," Audrey says, leaning around her daughter to grab a strawberry.

"Like you." Emily picks up another strawberry and hands it to her mom.

"My daddy is crazy busy finishing his album," Fleur says, already on to her fourth pancake. "It's going to be awesome."

The girls love hanging out at the studio with the guys. Sometimes Dillon takes them there on the weekend when they're not on such a tight deadline. It is housed on the grounds of Dillon's old home. He ended up completely remodeling the place after they moved the label to a trendy high-rise in downtown L.A. Now the house is a fully equipped commercial recording studio with several plush apartments on the grounds so bands signed to the label can live and work there in privacy. He added a new bar, enlarged game room, inside pool with a sauna and jacuzzi, and a state-of-the-art gym. It's like a mini luxury resort for rock stars, and it's a big hit with his artists.

"He wanted Mommy to sing on it, but she said no." Melody makes a face at me. "Daddy would be sooooo happy if you sing with him, Mommy. Please do it." She glues her hands together and lifts them up in a pleading gesture, tilting her head back and fixing me with big doe eyes. "Daddy would love you forever if you did it."

Ever since Dillon, Jamie, and Alex set up our *Grease*-inspired karaoke the night of Halloween, the kids have been begging me to sing on the album. The guys decorated the room with themed memorabilia and banners, and they set up a makeshift stage. We all took turns singing, individually and as couples, and the girls got a huge kick out of watching me and Dillon sing together.

Dillon being Dillon, he used it to his advantage, recruiting the girls to help in his campaign to get me to sing on the latest Collateral Damage album. My husband has been trying to get me to sing on a track since Vegas, but I repeatedly tell him that was a one-time thing.

"Daddy already loves Mommy forever," Fleur says, looking at me with a big, dreamy expression on her face. "When I grow up, I'm going to marry a rock star just like my Daddy and make smoochy faces at him all the time just like you do, Mommy."

Audrey snorts out a laugh. "What's a smoochy face?" she asks as warmth floods my chest, briefly eradicating the constant pain.

Fleur smiles and widens her eyes, tilting her head to the side and staring dreamily into space.

"I do not look like that!" I protest, smothering a laugh.

Audrey giggles, and my lips twitch.

"Just like that, Auntie Rey." Fleur straightens up and returns to stuffing herself with pancakes.

"I think you might have a little actress in the making," Audrey says.

"I think you might be right." Our eldest daughter is definitely theatrical, but Melody is too. Easton loves drama as well, and I wonder if any of them, or all of them, will follow Mom and Reeve into acting.

"I'm going to be a singer," Melody announces. "And I will sing with my daddy on every track."

"Daddy would love that," I say, darting down to press a kiss to her soft cheek. Both our girls have Dillon wrapped around their little fingers. He adores them as much as they adore him.

My husband is an amazing father. He somehow manages to be both playful and strict. If I want the kids to do anything, I usually have to ask repeatedly and raise my voice for anyone to take me seriously. Yet Dillon only has to say it once, in his stern disciplinarian voice, and they jump to obey. Even though he's the fun one, I'm actually softer. Together, it works, and we get the balance right.

Or we used to.

These days, I don't know if we're getting much right at all.

"Mom." Melody looks up at me with her big blue eyes, flinging her arms around my neck. "Please sing with my daddy. He loves you sooooo much, and you're the best singer and the best mommy in the whole wide world."

Her words bring tears to my eyes, and she can't know how much I need to hear and feel her love.

"Do it, Mom." Fleur clings to my arm and peers up at me with a matching pleading expression. She is the only one of my children to have my hazel eyes. The other three all have their fathers' blue eyes.

In the face of such devotion to Dillon and the excitement I know it will ignite, I relent. "My two princesses have convinced me." I kiss both their cheeks. "I'll do it. We can tell Daddy together when he gets home tonight."

There is much celebration and cries to call Dillon and tell him immediately, but I know they are busy now that Ro is back from Ireland and they can finish the album, so I don't want to disturb him.

Chapter Eleven
Vivien

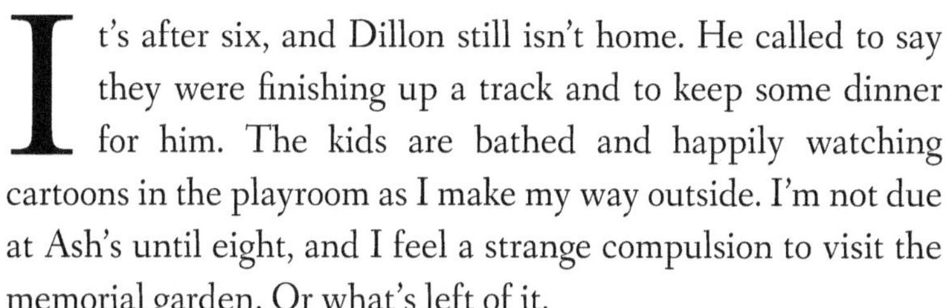

It's after six, and Dillon still isn't home. He called to say they were finishing up a track and to keep some dinner for him. The kids are bathed and happily watching cartoons in the playroom as I make my way outside. I'm not due at Ash's until eight, and I feel a strange compulsion to visit the memorial garden. Or what's left of it.

The flowers Dillon ordered arrived a few hours ago, coinciding with Bodhi's emergence from his room. It's the one and only time I have seen him today, and I stupidly saw it as a sign. I asked him to help me to replant the garden. I thought it might help him to remember and to begin to heal, but I should've known it was asking too much too soon.

I'm grasping at straws now. I'm terrified I'm losing my son forever, and I can't cope. I can't stand it. I can't bear to watch him self-destruct knowing I am powerless to do anything to stop it.

Pain lances through my chest as I hurry across the grass, rubbing at the pain as if that will make it go away. My path is guided by the illumination from the moon hanging low in the dark night sky.

I saw a flicker of something in Bodhi's eye when I asked, but it was gone so fast I can't be sure it wasn't wishful thinking. He shook his head and returned to his room without uttering a word.

"My heart is broken, Reeve," I say when I reach the cordoned-off area. I hop over Dillon's makeshift fence and plonk my butt down on the bench. I'm grateful Bodhi only flipped it over, that he hadn't broken it. The plaques nailed to the bark are intact as is the tree. Those are the most important parts. The rest we can replace, but I refuse to do it until Bodhi is ready to replant the garden.

When we moved to our new home in the Hollywood Hills, we had the tree professionally relocated from our old home. As a family, we planted this garden, and it meant something to me. Which is why I refuse to replant it until every member of our family participates. I don't care how long I have to wait.

"Help me. Help us!" I beseech, tipping my head back and looking at the smattering of stars lighting up the sky. "We love him. We love him as much as we love Fleur, Easton, and Melody. He's our son. He owns an equal part of our hearts. He's an integral part of our family. He's the only part of you still with me, but it's way more than that. I love him for the person he is. I love the quiet introspection he gives to every decision. I love the intensity on his handsome face when he's scribbling songs in his journal or playing his guitar. I love the adoration in his gaze when he watches his sisters and the joyful laugh he emits when he chases them around the playground. I love the respect shining in his eyes when he speaks with Dillon and the fierce way he protects his brother when Easton doesn't even notice it. I love his intelligence and his fight and his focus. I love how he hugs me. I love when he calls me Mom."

A sob tears from my throat, rippling through the still night air. "He's the sweetest boy, Reeve. You would have been so proud of him, and you'd be so worried now if you knew how messed up he is. A lot of that is your fault, and I'm pissed at you, but I can't get mad at you without turning that lens around on myself. I have tried to be the best mother to him and Easton, to my daughters too, but I'm failing. I'm failing my boys. They are both floundering, and I don't know how to help them!"

Tears spill from my eyes and I let them fall even though it feels like I've shed enough tears to fill an ocean recently. "Easton will be okay. I know he will. It doesn't stop me worrying about him, but I know he'll get through this. With Bodhi, I am genuinely terrified, Reeve. I know he is still the same sweet boy deep down inside. I know he is hurting and lashing out, but I'm so scared."

I get up and walk to the tree, running my finger over Reeve's name carved in the wood before doing the same with Lainey's. "I can't lose him too, and I'm fearful he's following a path he won't return from. It's a path I can't follow, and that hurts so bad. I'm supposed to hold my kids' hands and be with them for everything. But I can't follow Bodhi down this particular path, and I am terrified. If anything happens to him, I will die!" Wracking sobs rip from my chest as I drop to my knees, pressing my brow to the bark. "Help him, Reeve. I know you're still out there. Please help our son. Help me and Dillon to do the right thing. Just...help."

A gentle breeze lifts strands of my hair, and the lightest touch sweeps across my cheek. I whip my head back as my breath stutters in my chest. My nostrils twitch as a familiar spicy scent tickles the back of my nose. Tears stream unbidden down my face as I bring my fingers to my cheek. "Reeve," I whisper, lifting my hand to my other cheek as I feel a light touch brush against it. "You're here." I tilt my head back, staring up at the stars as the breeze wraps around me, cocooning me in the illusion of safety. Warmth infiltrates my body as I half laugh, half cry, surrounded by the ghosts of my past.

Some might think I'm crazy, but kneeling in the ruined garden, with memories of my first love playing in my head and the feel of his love winding around me, I feel at peace for the first time in weeks.

"I think your brother is considering having me committed," I joke a few hours later, stretching along Ash's comfy velvet couch as I knock back another glass of wine.

"Nonsense." Ash kicks her feet up on her coffee table. "He knows you used to feel Reeve around, and he made his peace with that a long time ago."

"I haven't felt him in years, Ash." I sit up a little straighter, turning on my side to face my sister-in-law. Audrey was supposed to be joining us for a girl's night in, but Lake and Kylo, her two-year-old twins, both came down with a fever this evening and she didn't want to leave them. "Do you think he's really there or is it my imagination conjuring him up at times of need?"

She shrugs, looking contemplative as she stares off into space. "The brain is a complex organ, and we still don't know enough about it. Perhaps it's a coping mechanism for times of high stress, or maybe he really is still there. If any man could stay anchored to the mortal realm, it would be Reeve Lancaster. That man was obsessed with you, and he loved you so fucking much. If there was a way to stay around you, I know he'd make it happen."

"Dillon has been incredible these past few weeks. I would be hanging from the cray-cray tree by my fingernails if it wasn't for your brother. I don't need Reeve to cope. I have Dillon."

"This has brought everything to the surface again. It's

understandable you might feel drawn to Reeve at a time like this."

"Something compelled me to go out to the garden tonight."

"Whether it was Reeve or your brain tricking you isn't really the issue though. What matters is it helped, right?"

"Yeah, it did, which is kind of silly, but—"

"Nope, not silly." She vigorously shakes her head. "Take the wins where you can, Viv, and don't ever feel bad for it."

"I love you," I tell her because it's the damn truth.

"I love you too." She grabs the bottle of wine and tops off both our glasses. "I know someone else who loves you extra special tonight."

I grin at her, and it's a miracle I can smile. "Let me guess. A tall, sexy, super talented rock star who is currently at my house with your husband and your brother perfecting the lyrics to the last track on the new Collateral Damage album, the one I am going to sing alongside him?"

"Ding, ding, ding!" She beams at me. "He was so excited when he called to tell me."

"I should have said yes years ago. I like making him happy. God knows we both need more of the happy stuff right now."

"Nope." She shakes her head and wags her finger in my face. "We're not going there tonight. You left your problems at the front door, remember?"

Thoughts of Bodhi and Easton instantly flood my mind, and it's hard to hold onto my previous happy thoughts when concern forces its way into my brain, but I try. I swore I wasn't going to be a Debbie Downer coming over here. "Right," I say with more determination than I feel.

"I love who my brother is when he's with you. Growing up, watching him battling his demons was so hard. All I ever wanted was for him to be happy and you make him so damn happy. I love the way you two love one another. It makes me want to break out into song whenever I see you making googly eyes at one another."

"You're ridiculous." I roll my eyes even though a massive grin spreads across my face. "But not wrong. I love the way your brother loves me." My expression turns more serious. "He loves me good, Ash, and I don't have the words to describe all the ways I love him back. I always wanted the kind of marriage my parents have, and I got it."

"Aww. I love that."

"You have your own epic kind of love too."

"I know." She beams from ear to ear. "We're lucky bitches."

"We are." I pull myself upright and knock back a mouthful of wine. "Have you given more consideration to adoption?" I ask because we haven't spoken about it for a while. Ever since this stuff blew up with the boys, I've been a bit of an absent friend.

"We're doing it."

"Oh my God!" I squeal, setting my glass down and hopping up. I run over and grab her into a hug. "That should have been the first thing out of your mouth tonight, instead of letting me ramble on about ghosts."

"You've had a lot on your mind."

"All the more reason to tell me. I'm so happy for your guys."

"Me too. Oisin is seven now, and we want to give him a brother or sister. We have tried everything to conceive again and it's time to accept it's not going to happen."

"You couldn't have tried harder." They have been through several rounds of IVF, attempted the surrogacy route, which turned into a disaster, and tried a couple of experimental procedures, none of which produced results. "You two have a lot of love to give so I'm thrilled you are adopting."

"Me too. It feels right, and the timing is perfect now."

"I need updates every step of the way." I grab my wine and

sit cross-legged on the floor beside her. "I don't care what shit is going on in my life, I want to know it all. You hear me?"

"You will know everything first. I promise."

"A toast," I say, raising my wineglass. "To families and kids and love, lots of love."

"Amen to all that."

We are in the kitchen making tea and toast a few hours later when Dillon walks into the house, instantly raising all my hackles.

"What's wrong?" I ask, spotting the panic he's trying to hide on his face.

"I got a call. Bodhi is in the hospital."

"Oh my God." My lower lip wobbles, and I sway on my feet. "Is he okay? Is he...alive?"

Dillon bands his arms around me and hugs me tight. "The nurse I spoke with said he was in surgery and he was stable."

"Surgery?" Ash asks, and I suspect her mind went to the same place mine did, but you don't need surgery if you've overdosed. At least, I don't think you do, but my brain is malfunctioning right now as panic races through my vein and blood thrums in my ears.

Pain is etched across Dillon's face as he tilts my chin up and looks me straight in the eye. "He was stabbed, sweetheart. That's as much as I know, but we've got to go."

"Take me to my son," I say, clinging to my husband as we race out of Ash's kitchen hond down the hallway.

Chapter Twelve
Bodhi

"A re the girls okay?" Mom asks in a hushed tone.

"They're fine. Jamie took them over to their place after breakfast. They'll keep them there as long as we need to stay here," my dad replies.

"I need him to wake up," my brother says in a tormented voice that hurts me. "The last words I said to him were horrible. I need him to know I take them back."

Pain rattles around my skull as I try to move my head, but it won't cooperate.

"He's going to be okay," Dad says. "You'll get a chance to tell him."

"So why isn't he waking up?" Easton says. "He's been out of surgery for hours."

Warmth spreads from my hand up my arm as I wage an inner war with my eyes, willing them to open. I try my body next, but my limbs refuse to move. Awareness creeps into my consciousness as pain radiates from my side, up over my chest, and higher. A painful tightness stretches across my ribs and around to my back, and I feel the darkness calling me back to slumber, but I don't want to sleep.

It all rushes back to me like a movie on fast-forward, and I want to wake. I need to tell my family I'm sorry and I love them.

"His body needs time to rest and heal." Mom's voice cracks, and a different kind of pain rips through me.

I caused that anguish in her voice. The anguish in all their voices. And I couldn't hate myself any more than I do in this moment.

My body jerks as I fight to regain consciousness.

"Bodhi." Mom's soft tone is like a comfort blanket swaddling me. "Honey, are you there? Can you hear me?"

I feel her hand squeezing mine as my eyes slowly blink open with an exhaustion that threatens to reclaim me if I don't fight it. My eyes shutter again as my fingers close around hers.

"Bro." Easton's voice sounds closer. "You're in the hospital, but you're going to be okay. The doc says you'll make a full recovery. It's okay to wake up. We're not mad at you."

"He is squeezing my hand," Mom says as I battle the tiredness and force my eyes to open again.

Slowly, my vision comes into focus, and I see Mom, Dad, and East all standing over me with concerned expressions on their faces.

It is so unbelievably good to see them. There was a point where I thought I never would again, and every horrible mistake I made flashed behind my eyes as I lay bleeding out on the dirty ground of the alley thinking I was dying.

"Mom," I croak as wetness seeps over my cheeks. "I'm sorry."

"Shush, honey." She brushes hair back off my face. "There is plenty of time for that. Don't worry about it now. Do you want some ice chips?"

I peer deep into her troubled face, and I hate I have caused her so much pain. It shouldn't have taken me almost dying to realize the truth. For weeks, I have struggled to clear the fog from my head and see what has always been right in front of me. I couldn't see it, hear it, or think it because I was consumed with pain, writhing in agony with every conscious moment I lived, and I just wanted it all to stop.

"I love you," I rasp, the words scraping over the raw ache in my throat and the dryness in my mouth. I move my head, looking at my dad and my brother. "I love you all, and I'm so sorry."

Mom's sobs filter into the solemn silence as her arms go gently around me and she cries against the side of my face.

Dad moves around my bed to comfort her. "We love you too, son," he says, his voice thick with emotion. "Thank fuck, you're going to be okay. You gave us quite a scare." He holds my hand as he rubs a soothing hand up and down Mom's back.

"I didn't mean what I said," Easton says, hovering by my other side.

I lift my gaze to his.

"I don't hate you. I never could. You're my brother. You mean more to me than some stupid girl who tried to come between us."

Shame washes over me as I think about all the nasty things I have said and done to East. He deserved none of them. He has always had my back, and it was a shitty way to repay him. But I'll make it up to him. I swear. "Bros before hoes," I croak, attempting to smile. "I'm sorry, East. That was a shitty thing to do. I wish I could take it back. I was just hurting so much, and I wanted you to feel some of that pain."

"I get it."

"You didn't deserve it. I know you liked her, and I'm sorry I ruined your relationship."

"I'm not. She had an agenda. I'm not going to say what you did was okay, because your betrayal cut deep, but in a weird way you actually protected me."

If I hadn't been so smashed and so determined to hurt my brother, that bullshit the bitch spewed would have made me seriously mad. At least we won't have to worry about Hollis coming between us again; her father has sent her to an all-girls reform school in Switzerland. An asshole at school recorded some of the events that night, and the video found its way into her father's inbox. He shipped her out of the country two days later. Can't say I'll miss her. She was nothing more than a tool to hurt my brother. A fresh wave of shame crashes into me and I hate what I did to East.

"Let's sit you upright a little so I can give you some of these ice chips. The nurse didn't leave any water, only these." Mom tenderly cups my face. "I'm so glad you're okay. We were so worried."

"I'll let the nurse know you're awake," Dad says, as East presses a button on the side of the bed and it slowly elevates. Dad leans down and kisses my brow. "It's good to have you back, son."

His words carry a double meaning, and they linger in the air as he leaves to get the nurse. The gentle whirring as the bed raises is the only sound in the room.

I am sitting propped up in the bed with Mom feeding me ice chips when Dad returns with a nurse. She makes a fuss over me, checking my vitals and promising to send a doctor in to talk to us and some food if he gives me the all-clear. She reappears a couple of minutes later with a large glass jug of water and some plastic cups. Mom holds my hand while she helps me to take small sips as if she is terrified to let me go.

I guess I fell asleep after that because when I blink my eyes open the room is brighter, and little rays of daylight filter through the gaps in the blinds.

"Hey." Mom's beautiful face swims in my line of vision as she looms over me. "How are you feeling?"

As soon as the words leave her lips, I'm acutely aware of all the aches and pains ricocheting through my body. "Sore," I truthfully admit. "Can you help me to sit up?"

"Let me," Dad says, and I move my head around, watching him enter the room holding two paper cups.

My brother is asleep in a chair alongside my bed, his head thrown back, his lips slightly parted as he softly snores. The sound is like music to my ears. For years, East and I shared a bedroom until we became teens and he started snoring, waking me continuously during the night, and it became apparent I needed to start sleeping in my own room. Occasionally, when we stay up late watching TV or playing video games, I crash in his room. It always reminds me of the closeness we share and how much of a support system he was for me when I first moved in with them and it felt like my entire world ended when Lori died.

Dad hands a cup to Mom before setting the other one down on the bedside table. Then he elevates the bed and fixes the pillows behind my back.

"Where am I?" I ask because I have no recollection after I passed out on the sidewalk outside the bar, having crawled from the alley.

"You're at Southern California Hospital at Culver City," Mom explains.

"What do you remember?" Dad takes his cup and sits beside Mom. They pull their chairs in closer to my bed.

"All of it." I wince a little as I sit up straighter in the bed. "Unfortunately."

The nurse shows up then to check me over, but I refuse her

offer of more pain meds for now. I want to talk to my parents and my brother. I have so many things I need to get off my chest and it can't wait any longer.

I have put them through hell, and I need to fix it now.

She leaves after promising to send a light breakfast in for me, but food is the last thing on my mind. East is still asleep, but I don't want to wake him or delay this conversation.

"Do you feel up to talking about it?" Dad asks, sipping his coffee as he watches me with laser-focused eyes. "The cops have been around, but they weren't able to tell us much other than you were found in front of a dive bar in West Adams, bleeding out and beaten up."

A strangled sound erupts from Mom's mouth, and tears glisten in her eyes. I squeeze her hand, only imagining what she must have felt when she heard the news.

Dad circles his arm around Mom and holds her close. I don't even know if he realizes he has done it. It just comes automatically to him. When I'm older, I hope I find someone to love as much as they love one another. It's couple goals for sure.

"They will be back to take a statement from you, most likely at some point today," Dad adds.

"You're awake," East says in a hoarse voice, and we all turn to look at him as he rubs sleep from his eyes.

"He just woke a few minutes ago." Mom stretches across the bed to hand him her undrunk coffee. "You look like you need this more than me."

"Thanks." He accepts it without protest, immediately taking a mouthful and forcing himself more upright in the chair.

A woman enters the room with a tray holding two pieces of toast, a glass of juice, and a Styrofoam bowl with some chopped fruit. Mom insists I eat all of it before I begin explaining. They fill me in on my sisters and how worried they were when they got the call from the hospital while I eat.

"I'm really sorry you were worried. I know I've been horrible to everyone." Tears prick my eyes, but I don't fight them. If I'm going to do this, I'm doing it right. That means no more shielding things from my family.

Dad removes my tray, setting it over by the window ledge before reclaiming his seat by Mom's side. Mom clings to one of my hands while my brother holds the other.

"It hurt so much," I whisper, my eyes blurry.

"We never should have made that movie," Mom says as tears roll down her cheeks.

"I'm glad you made the movie," I truthfully tell her, unsurprised to see shock materialize on her face. I squeeze her hand. "It wasn't a secret that Reeve gave me up, Mom. I've known that since Lori told me the truth, but I purposely didn't think about it until the movie forced me to."

Agony transforms her beautiful face, and I push on even though it's hard for me to talk about this stuff with anyone. But I owe it to my parents, to my brother, to tell them the raw truth, no matter how much it might hurt to hear some of this stuff.

I thought I was going to die and I'd never get to tell them these things, so I'm not chickening out now.

"This was always bound to happen, Mom." I brush the tears from her cheeks. "What happened recently has been years in the making."

"It is better we heard the truth through your eyes, as the people who lived it, rather than the shit that's on the internet," East agrees.

I nod. "East is right. The movie put some things into perspective, but it still hurt. It forced me to confront things I have tried to bury. I'm embarrassed I didn't handle it well. Instead of pushing you away, I should have confided in you, but my head was a mess. It still is. All these thoughts keep going round and round in my brain and they are driving me mad. I was so angry at everyone for lying to me, and then I got angry at myself for believing you took me in as anything other than pity. I couldn't get it all to stop, and I just wanted it to stop." I fist my hand in the bedsheet and avert my eyes. "Numbing the thoughts and the pain with booze and drugs was the only thing that worked."

I lift my eyes slowly, knowing what I will see when I look at my parents and my brother. "I couldn't talk to you. All I saw when I looked at you was pity and guilt, and I hated that." I eyeball my brother. "All I could see when I looked at you was everything I wasn't. He chose you. My dad picked *you* over me. I have always felt like I've been in your shadow. You are amazing at everything and one of the best people I know. I could live a million lifetimes and never be as good as you."

"Bo, that is so wrong. We're different people, but it doesn't make you better or worse than me. You're a good person too. I'm sorry if I ever made you feel like you weren't. You're my brother. The best brother a guy could have. If I've done stuff to make you think you're in my shadow, I am so fucking sorry. That's not how I feel. It's not how I want *you* to feel."

Tears well in his eyes and it pains me to have hurt my brother. I squeeze his hand. "It's not your fault. You have never done anything to make me feel inferior. No one has." I look over at my parents. "You have treated me fairly and equally and with so much love. The way I feel is on *me*. It's not because of anything any of you have done. Please believe me."

Chapter Thirteen
Bodhi

"We love you so much, Bodhi," Mom says through her tears. "When Lori first came to see me and your dad and she told us about you, we were in total shock. I didn't know if I could love Saffron's child."

Agony is etched upon her face, and I know it's hard for her to say these things to me, but I appreciate her honesty. It's not anything I don't know from the movie now anyway.

"We spent a week talking and reflecting on it, running through our options," Dad explains.

He runs a hand through his bleach-blond hair, and the strain on his face is obvious. The scruff on his chin is thicker than he usually wears it, and he has dark shadows and pronounced bags under his eyes. He looks exhausted. I know him, and I bet he didn't sleep because he wanted Mom and Easton to sleep, and he watched over me in case I woke.

"We independently reached the decision to adopt you because we wanted to give you a home, Bodhi. We wouldn't have reached that decision if we couldn't have treated you as an equal member of this family." Dad leans over and grips the side of my head with a gentle touch. "My flesh and blood runs through your veins, Bodhi. You're as much my son as Easton is. It kills me that you would ever think that couldn't be true." He presses his brow to mine for few seconds before easing back, not wanting to hurt me, I'm guessing. "Having you in my life helped to assuage some of my guilt with regards to Reeve. I never got a chance to know my brother. Some of that was my fault, and it's something I must live with for the rest of my life. I have made my peace with it because continuing to beat myself up over something that is in the past, something I can't control or change, is pointless. It took me years to accept that realization, so I understand some of what you're going through. Getting to raise Reeve's son was a way for me to feel connected to him, but, my God, Bodhi, you are so much more than that."

Tears drip down his face as he reclaims his seat, placing his hand over Mom's hand on mine. Mom is still crying too, and Easton is swiping at a few errant tears leaking from his eyes.

Hell, I'm an emotional mess as well.

But that's nothing new.

What is new is the fact I'm not hiding it anymore.

"You are *my son*, and I love you for the person you are. Not because you are Reeve's son or a way for me to connect with the brother I didn't know. Like your brother said, you're a good person. Smart, compassionate, caring. I watch you jotting down song lyrics in your journal, and my heart bursts with pride knowing we share the same passion. I listen to you composing songs on your guitar in the studio and I'm blown away by your talent and your commitment. I see how you dote on your sisters, look up to your brother, and every time you call Vivien Mom, I feel it in here." He thumps a hand over his chest.

"I cried tears of joy the first time you called me Mommy," Mom says. "I was pregnant with Fleur, and it was about four or five months after Lori passed. We were really worried about you. You were so quiet. You kept so much locked up inside. You called me Mommy Vivien, and I seriously thought my heart would burst."

She leans in and kisses my cheek. "Like Dillon, at first, I thought adopting you would be a way for me to keep a piece of Reeve with me always, and it is. Some days, you say something a certain way, or make a gesture that reminds me of your father, and it takes me back." She looks over at Easton. "I see reminders of Reeve in you too. You both look so alike it's not hard to see it at times." She kisses my dad on the lips. "I see elements of you in the boys too."

He kisses her back, nodding.

She returns her attention to me. "But, Bodhi, you are so much more than that. It's like Dillon said, you're your own person. A truly wonderful, amazing, inquisitive, thoughtful, deep thinker. Watching you blossom and grow has been one of the most rewarding experiences of my life." She reaches across the bed for Easton's hand. "That goes for you as well. We are so blessed with both you boys and we love you very much." A cry filters from her lips. "It kills me to think you might not feel that."

"No, Mom." Ignoring the searing-hot pain the motion produces, I lean forward and hug her. "You have done nothing wrong. I know you love me. It's me who feels unworthy of all of you, not the other way around."

Dad and Easton sit on the edge of the bed, carefully draping their arms around us as we embrace in a group hug.

And it's everything.

It would be virtually impossible for me to ignore their love when they surround me with it all the time. Even when I was putting them through hell, they never gave up on me.

"I hate that you feel unworthy," Mom says when we break our embrace and everyone reclaims their seats. She softly cups my cheek. "You are so worthy, Bodhi, and we are lucky to have you in our lives." She peers at me with so much love in her eyes it would be impossible to deny the truth. "I know you have a lot of emotions to process. I know the things you have to deal with are things no boy your age should ever have to face. But you aren't alone. You have us. We will help you to get through this. But please don't shut us out again. Let us help you. Let us love you. Let us be there for you the way a family should, because we love you and we hate to see you in so much pain."

"I know it won't be easy," Dad says, piercing me with that no-bullshit look of his. "I went through something similar when I was your age, and I can relate to some of how you are feeling. We can't make this right for you. You need to process this yourself, and you are going to get mad, sad, and every other emotion in between. Just promise us you'll lean on us. You can talk to me at any time about anything, and I won't judge."

He leans back, exhaling with a wry smile. "I was an absolute asshole back in the day. I treated my parents like shit. I didn't tell my mum I loved her until I was in my twenties. I lashed out at everyone, and I fixated on revenge instead of trying to heal myself. If my mistakes can help you to avoid making the same ones, I will gladly tell you everything. But only you can do the hard work, buddy. We will support you however we can, but the hard slog is yours. It won't be easy and there is no quick fix."

"You are entitled to your feelings, Bodhi," Mom adds, dabbing at her face with a tissue. "Just like East is entitled to his." Her gaze dances between us. "Both of you need to work through them. Don't ever feel guilty for how you feel but let us help you figure it out."

"I will try," I admit, meaning it with my whole heart, as East bobs his head.

"Why were you in West Adams?" Mom asks. "I need to

understand how you ended up there and who did this to you because those assholes are going to be behind bars even if I have to scour the streets searching for them myself." Fierce determination glimmers in her eyes along with righteous anger.

"Steady on there, GI Jane," Dad says, his lips tipping up at the corners. "You won't be stepping foot in that hellhole. We'll hire a PI and find these scumbags ourselves, doling out some vigilante justice of our own before we hand them on a silver platter to the cops." His eyes burn as he stares at me. "Mark my words, those assholes will pay for this."

"Yes, Dad." Easton nods in agreement. "I want in on the vigilante justice part. Those fuckers hurt my brother, and I want to make them pay." He cracks his knuckles, looking ready to bulldoze the world for me.

A lump wedges in my throat. How could I ever have thought the things I thought about my family? All they have ever done is love me and take care of me. I know I have a long road ahead to deal with things, but I make a silent vow to myself to not take it out on my family anymore.

They are the heroes in my story. They are not my enemy.

"I saw you out in the garden," I blurt, staring at Mom. "I heard some of the things you said. I heard you begging Reeve to help." The lump thickens in my throat, and I swallow painfully. "I couldn't handle it. Knowing how much I was hurting you, and I was so confused. I needed to know more about the past. To see it with my own eyes, so I took the spare truck keys, drove out to San Jose, and I visited the house I lived at with Lori." I rub at the tight pain in my chest that has nothing to do with my physical injuries. "I can hardly remember her anymore," I admit in a low voice.

"I can relate." East leans forward in his chair. "I barely remember Reeve anymore. The memories I have are fleeting and fading."

My natural instinct is to lash out, to tell him at least he still has some memories. Or even if he doesn't, it doesn't wipe out the fact he had five years with my father when I got no time with him.

But I force that instinct aside. It's not my brother's fault that happened. The blame squarely lies with Reeve and Reeve alone. He made that decision, and he's the only one who deserves my scorn and my hatred, so I promise myself I will direct all that aggression and hostility in his direction. I won't blame my parents or Easton for Reeve's sins.

"Lori loved you so much, Bodhi," Mom says. "She was in a lot of pain those last few months, but she worked tirelessly to ensure you were taken care of before she died. She was a great mother and you adored her."

"I have been mad at her for abandoning me too, which is unfair when it wasn't her fault."

"You can't force yourself to feel a certain way and emotions are there to be felt and understood. It seems like you have dealt with that one," Dad says.

"I'm not sure I have dealt with any, but things are starting to look a little clearer. I just wish it hadn't taken a near-death experience to reach this point."

"You're alive, and you'll make a full recovery. You have some cracked ribs, a mild concussion, and the gash on your side is nasty, and it'll leave a scar, but the knife missed all your vital organs," Mom reassures me, patting my hand.

"The doctors cleaned the wound and stitched it, and they have you on antibiotics, as well as pain meds, to ward off infection. You should be allowed to go home in a couple of days," Dad says.

"That's good, but I wish I could leave now. I miss my sisters. I want to hug them and tell them I love them too."

"We can bring them over later," Dad says. "I know they'd like to see you."

"I'd like that." I clear my throat, and Mom instantly reaches for my water. I take a few sips before continuing, knowing this part is going to devastate my parents. "I wanted to know more about Saffron," I blurt, watching Mom's face pale and Dad's arm automatically go around her shoulders. "I needed to know she wasn't all bad because if she's all bad there's a good chance I'm the same too, right? I mean, neither of my parents were saints, and both were addicts."

"Your father beat his addiction, and you will too." Mom's voice resonates with supreme confidence, and I hope I am strong enough to not let her down. "And there isn't a bad bone in your body, Bodhi. You have always been a good kid."

"Being troubled doesn't equate to being bad," Dad says.

"But the choices you make from here on out will largely dictate that," Easton says, sounding way older than he is. But that's my brother. "You lost your way, bro, but you'll find it back."

"What did you do?" Mom asks, chewing on the corner of her lip.

"I found a guy online who went to school with Saffron. I had reached out to him, and he suggested meeting up. I wasn't sure if I wanted to go there, but after hearing you in the garden, I knew I needed to find out if I was to have any chance to move beyond this. I met him at Lori's and Saffron's childhood home. It was in a shitty neighborhood, and the house is abandoned now. It was all boarded up and overrun with weeds."

That was the first wake-up call. Staring at the poverty they grew up in showed me how fortunate I was to have grown up in nice neighborhoods never wanting for any material thing. "I actually felt kind of sorry for her," I truthfully admit. "It's like she never stood a chance."

"Saffron had plenty of chances," Mom says. "She threw them all away including an acting career and all the money she made from it."

"And Lori grew up there, and she was a decent person," Dad adds. "We all have choices in life, like Easton just alluded to. No matter our circumstances, the decisions we make shape the people we become and the lives we lead. I'm so fucking lucky I got the opportunity to make up for my mistakes, and I choose to live my life more openly now. Not everyone gets that chance. I'm grateful I had so many people around me who cared enough to help set me straight. You do too, Bodhi."

"I know," I whisper, biting on the inside of my mouth. "I was clutching at straws, wanting to see something good in her, but there is none." My voice sounds hollow to my own ears as I continue. "Dirk took me to the bar. He said there were some other guys there who knew Saffron." I gulp back bile. "They were cool at first, and we shared beers. But gradually the masks came off, and I saw them for what they were."

My chest heaves, and I squeeze my eyes shut as I remember all the horrible stuff they said about my bio mom. I know they weren't lying, but I didn't need to know all the gory details. I was trying to cling to an illusion she was a drug addict who was incapable of making any decision when it came to her child, but the truth is, Saffron Roberts was a cold, heartless, selfish bitch her entire life. It wasn't the drugs that made her like that. It was just her.

"They said horrible things about her," I admit, forcing my eyes open. "But it wasn't lies. They told stories of week-long drug and booze orgies where they all shared her. She routinely broke up relationships, and she had at least three abortions those guys knew of." A shuddering breath escapes my lips as I pause to take a minute. This shit is hard to say.

"You don't have to continue if it's too painful for you, honey," Mom says.

"Yes, he does," Dad counteracts. "If Bodhi is serious about facing up to his issues, he can't bury his head in the sand any longer."

"He's lying on a hospital bed, bruised, stabbed, and concussed, Dil," Mom replies. "We can cut him some slack until he feels better."

"No." I shake my head. "Dad is right, Mom. There'll be no ideal time to face up to this shit. Hiding behind my injuries is no different than hiding behind my shame and my fear." I rub her arm. "I'm okay. I want to get this all out."

"I'm here for you," East says, his voice projecting strength. Strength I know I'll need to lean on in the coming months.

"It became clear I'd made a big mistake," I continue. "A few of the guys turned nasty, and they told me Saffron had OD'd owing them money. It was obvious they expected me to repay her debts and I'd been baited into a trap. I tried to run. Got outside to my truck when they caught up to me. They hauled me into an alley and started punching and kicking me. I tried to fight back but there were six of them and only one of me. I'd brought a knife with me."

I'm not completely stupid or confused to the point I didn't care at all about my safety. Though I've been going around acting like I have a death wish, deep down I have never wanted to die. I just wanted the noise in my head to stop. The pain in my heart to go away.

"I tried to use it to get away, but they overpowered me, took the knife, and one of the guys stabbed me with it. The other assholes went crazy. They knew who I was. They knew they would get heat if anything happened to me."

"It still didn't stop them from leaving you there," Mom says, and her voice sounds all choked up again.

Dad kisses her temple and wraps his arms more tightly around her.

"They panicked and ran," I explain. "They stole my truck, my wallet, my cell, and they took Reeve's golf watch." I can't look at her as I admit the last part. I know my parents won't care about the truck, my cell, or the wallet. They are replaceable, but Reeve's watch isn't.

"What?" Easton blurts, looking confused, and I guess he hadn't noticed it was missing from the top drawer of his bedside table. "Why did you have my watch when you have your own?"

After I came to live with my family, Mom gave me some things of Reeve's. She had given Easton some after he died, and she wanted me to have a few of his treasured items too. She gave me the watch she bought him on his twenty-fifth birthday, but I always secretly wanted the golf watch as she gave it to him when he was seventeen and he barely took it off. I know because I've seen it on him in so many of the photos in the albums Mom keeps in the living room.

"I stole the watch from your room."

Easton stares at me in shock.

"It was an asshole move." I eyeball my brother, hoping he can see the genuine remorse on my face. "I know how much you loved that watch, so I stole it to fuck with your head. I honestly don't know why I wore it that day. Something compelled me to put it on. I begged them not to take it when they untied it from my wrist. I knew it would devastate you and Mom to lose it. I'm so sorry, East."

His Adam's apple bobs in his throat, and it guts me when he looks away. Mom has a hand over her mouth, and I hate I have disappointed her again.

"It's okay," Easton says after a few beats of silence.

"No, it's not."

"Your life is worth more than a watch, Bo."

"Reeve would say the same if he were here," Mom says.

"This is going to sound hella crazy, but I think...I think he was there with me in the alley."

You could hear a pin drop in the room. Dad and East look shocked as hell, but Mom is smiling. "I don't think that's crazy, honey. You know I used to feel him around me in the aftermath of his death. I haven't sensed his presence for a long time. I don't know if you stuck around in the garden to see, but I felt him that night. I was crying to him for help, and he answered." Tears roll down her face again. "What did you experience?"

My heart is beating superfast, thumping against my rib cage, adrenaline coursing through my veins at the thought my bio dad might have actually been with me in some way. My mind wanders back to that night. "I was on the ground in the alley, and the wound in my side was gushing blood. I had my hands pressed to it, but it wouldn't stop bleeding."

I look down at my hospital gown, placing my palm over the bandaged wound. "I tried to get up. I knew I needed to get back out onto the street, or I would die in that alley because no one would've found me in the dark in time to save me." I draw a deep breath. "I couldn't get up. My legs wouldn't cooperate. I think it was a combination of shock and blood loss." I wet my dry lips. "Then I heard someone in my ear urging me to get up, telling me to fight. I went rigidly still, looking around in confusion for the owner of the voice, but there was no one there."

Mom is practically bouncing in her seat, and Dad is as white as a ghost—no pun intended. Easton looks riveted and intrigued.

"Then I felt someone nudging me. Reeve's image popped into my mind, and I freaked. I'm not sure I connected the dots at first, but I was scared enough that it jolted my body into action. I managed to get to my feet, and I hobbled out of there as fast as I could. The last thing I remember is collapsing in front of a couple on the sidewalk before I passed out."

"Oh my God. Oh my God." Mom repeats it over and over again before a laugh bubbles up her throat. She leans in and kisses me before doing the same to Easton and Dillon. Then she graces us with the biggest smile. "Reeve listened. He helped you." She clasps both my cheeks, taking care to be gentle. "Your father saved you, Bodhi. He came through for you when you needed him."

Epilogue
DILLON – 18 months later

"A re you crying?" Vivien whispers, leaning into my side as she scrutinizes my face.

"Yes," I readily admit, circling my arm around her slender shoulders. "I'm so fucking proud of our boys and secure enough in my manhood that I can cry in public and own up to it."

"God, I love the hell out of you, Dillon Lancaster O'Donoghue." She stretches up and smacks a loud kiss on my lips. When she pulls back, she's grinning. "I'm secure enough in our love and proud of the husband and father you are to kiss you in public and not give a flying fuckity-fuck who saw or what they think about it."

"That's my girl." I slap her ass.

I feel disapproving, disbelieving eyes around us, and I'm tempted to flip them the bird, but that would be immature. Considering I'll be forty in eight months, I figure I should probably try to act my age. Besides, it's our sons high-school graduation, and nothing should steal their thunder.

The long ceremony ends, thank fuck, and our boys make their way over to us.

"I'm so proud of you," Vivien squeals, flinging her arms around both boys and hugging them to death. "I love you, I love you, I love you." She peppers their faces with kisses, and both boys wear similar amused adoring grins. They love their mother, and it makes me happy to know it and see it.

"Control your woman," Easton teases, eyeballing me over Viv's shoulder when she shows no sign of stopping.

"Women should never be controlled, son." I reel Viv back into my arms. "You should only ever want to free their wings and give them room to fly."

"Spoken like a true poet," Bodhi says, grinning at me.

"Takes one to know one." I waggle my brows as another surge of pride swells in my chest. "I won't be the only fool in our house writing love songs for a living. Come Monday, that accolade will be passed to you."

"Now, I feel left out," Easton pouts.

"Don't talk stupid." Bodhi wraps his arm around East's neck, grinning. "You're going to play ball for the Bears. I'm proud of you little brother."

"Hey. I'm not the little one in this combo." East wrangles out of his hold, straightening up and puffing out his chest as he wags his finger in Bodhi's face. He has a couple of inches in height over Bodhi, and he's much broader and more muscular too. He loves to tease his brother over it any chance he gets. "And we're both eighteen now."

"I'm still six months older than you. Last I checked that makes me the eldest and you the little brother."

"You two would fight over air," Viv says, fiddling with the settings on her Nikon. She insisted on bringing the big guns out today.

"Are we going to the restaurant yet?" Fleur asks, looking

bored. She turned ten on her last birthday, and she's already entered the tween phase. God help us all.

"I want to get some photos of the boys with their friends and then we'll leave."

"Auntie Ash is outside," I say, mussing up my eldest daughter's hair. Predictably, she scowls at me, before rushing to fix it. "You can join her and wait there for us," I suggest.

"I'll come too," Melody says, instantly threading her fingers in her sister's.

"We'll walk them out," Lauren offers, beaming at her granddaughters. "Just give me one second to congratulate your brothers." She moves over to hug Easton and Bodhi.

Fleur grumbles, deepening the sound when Jonathon musses up her hair again.

We share a chuckle and a knowing look. My father-in-law and I have grown very close over the years, and he's a man I admire a hell of a lot. Lauren and Jon now spend half the year in Italy, at the home Reeve bequeathed them in his will. We joined them for a few months last summer, and it did wonders for Bodhi's mood.

Our boy has tried hard to deal with the ghosts of his past this last eighteen months. It hasn't been plain sailing. He relapsed at the start of senior year, but he came and told us, allowing us to get him the support he needed. We discussed him going into rehab, but Bodhi didn't want to defer senior year, so he attended an outpatient program for a couple of months around school, and he managed to get through it and graduate on time with his brother. Something which was important to him.

Bodhi is itching to leave school behind him and come work with me at the label. He has no desire to be front and center stage, but he wants to learn the industry from the ground up and he wants to be a songwriter and producer. He certainly has the talent, and I couldn't be more excited he is joining the CD label next week.

Lauren and Jonathon leave with our girls while Viv gets the boys to pose for her.

"Why is Ash outside, or do I want to know?" she asks as she snaps some pics.

"Did you really expect my sister to wait patiently at the restaurant for us to arrive? You know she adores these guys. Hell if I know why," I joke, flashing them a grin. I'm deflecting on purpose. The whole O'Donoghue clan is outside, having flown in from Ireland to be here to celebrate with us. I wanted to surprise everyone, so I made my sister and Jamie keep it a secret.

"Funny, Dad. Not." East nudges me in the ribs, and I tackle him playfully.

Viv takes a ton more photos, grabbing some of the guys' friends into pictures. Lewis's mom takes a few shots of the four of us together, and then I finally manage to get Vivien to leave. Ash has been blowing up my phone the last fifteen minutes. My sister is not known for her patience.

We walk out of the dwindling auditorium together with my hand wrapped around Vivien's and one son on either side of us. When we reach the hallway, I stop them before we head outside to complete bedlam. My Irish family are not known for being subtle or quiet, but I wouldn't have them any other way.

It took me a long time to appreciate the value of family, and now I have so many different variations of family and so many people I love. I never take it for granted.

"Stop for a second," I say, moving us over to the side. "I want to say something before we go outside."

"Oh damn. Dad's about to get totes emote. Prepare yourself," East says, snaking his arm around his brother's shoulder.

I am glad they were able to put that horrible stuff behind

them and repair their relationship. If anything, I think they are even closer now.

These next few years will be a test of their bond as they each make their own way in the world.

Easton is going to live on campus, like Viv did, but we aren't far away, so I expect we'll still see a lot of him. Easton is a home bird at heart, and he loves his family too much to not make time for us.

Bodhi has chosen to stay at home for now, and we were both relieved to hear it. Though he has made a lot of progress, he is still not out of the woods. We want him close, so we can continue to support him. It helps to soften the blow too. Our boys are grown up and spreading their wings. It's a confusing time full of joy at the men they are becoming and the paths they are forging in life, and sadness because they are moving on and leaving home and we're going to miss them.

"You're not too old to knock the shit out of," I joke, narrowing my eyes at my son. "Punk," I add, so he knows I'm just messing.

"Get on with it, Dad. We've got dinner and a party to get to," East retorts.

"I just want to say your mother and I are super fucking proud of you both. It's an honor to be your parents. Watching you grow up has been a privilege and the most rewarding experience of our lives. I know things haven't always been easy, but you've faced your challenges head on, and we love you both very much." I grip Bodhi's shoulder and then East's.

"No matter how old you get, we are always your family," Viv says, emotion threading through her tone. "We are always here for you, for anything you need."

"Like condoms," I quip, lightening the mood.

"Dillon!" Viv thumps me in the arm.

"What?" I hold up my hands and plant an innocent expression on my face. "We should encourage them to wrap it before they tap it."

"Oh God." Viv buries her face in my neck. "I do not want to think about my babies' sex lives."

"Ugh, Mom. That sounds so wrong," East says as Bodhi and I share a grin.

Viv lifts her head and grabs Easton's cheeks, smushing them together. "You will always be my baby, Easton." She lets his face go to grab Bodhi's in the same way. "You too, Bodhi." Releasing his face, she slides back into my arms where she belongs. "Even when you're fifty, you'll still be my babies. And we will always be here for you."

"Always." I pull the boys into a group hug, holding them close. "Family forever."

"Family forever," they chorus as one.

It's a mantra I will follow with my whole heart and soul until the day I die.

***

Reeve, a companion novel to *Say I'm the One* and *Let Me Love You* is AVAILABLE NOW in eBook, Kindle Unlimited, paperback, hardcover and audio. Turn the page to read a sample.

Vivien Grace Mills has been the center of my universe since the second she entered this world.

Every memory I hold precious includes her.

She's my biggest champion and the one person keeping me sane during some of the most testing times of my life.

Vivien shows me what it means to love and be loved.

I know she's *the one* from an early age.

When I land my dream role, plans for our future are finally coming true.

Until everything falls apart, leaving a complicated trail of broken, scarred hearts and long-lasting consequences.

I messed up: I failed her. I failed *me.*

I won't rest until the only woman I love is back in my arms.

Nothing or no one will stop me from reclaiming her heart.

Not my manipulative costar, my greedy agent, or the backstabbing studio publicist.

And especially not *him*.

My determination and patience are successful, and Vivien is back where she belongs.

I finally have the family I have craved my entire life.

But I sacrificed so much for my poor decisions, and I'm not finished paying the price.

THEN – age 6

"Stay right here." Beth points at Viv and me, trying to look scary, but it doesn't work. My best friend smiles sweetly, waving as her nanny leaves the room with her cell phone pressed to her ear. Her boyfriend is always calling her when Viv's parents go out. Lauren would be mad if she knew. But Viv doesn't want to snitch because we get away with lots of stuff when Beth isn't looking.

"Come on." Viv grins as she tugs on my arm. "The workers are gone. Let's check out the treehouse."

I shake my head and hold her wrist. "Your dad said we weren't to go out in the garden." Jonathon left to drive Lauren to the airport. She's going to Ireland for her movie premiere. Vivien begged her to let us go with her, but she said we couldn't miss school.

"Reeve." Viv puts her hands on her hips and gives me that look. The one that says she's the boss and I'm to do what she wants or else. "Daddy will be gone for ages. We'll be back inside before Beth even knows."

"It's dangerous," I say, looking out the window at the area at the top of the garden where the men are building our new treehouse. Last year, they built an obstacle course, and before that, they built the playground Viv and I play in every day. I know it's going to be mega, and I can't wait. But I don't want to get in trouble. Mr. Mills said we weren't to go near it, and he'll be angry if we do. I don't want him to tell me I can't come over anymore because I hate my house.

I hate my daddy.

Well, not really. He's my daddy. I love him even if he's

always shouting at me. "And my dad will be mad if he finds out."

Vivien scowls. "Your daddy is mean! Who cares what he thinks."

I do. "He'll shout at me."

"Then I'll kick his ass!" Vivien balls her hands into fists, looking like she's ready to go into battle with my daddy.

A weird fluttery feeling spreads across my chest. "We'll just wait until your daddy comes back, and then we'll ask him to take us out to see it."

Vivien's long dark hair falls around her shoulders as she shakes her head. "It will be too dark then." She looks over her shoulder out the window. "It's already starting to get dark now." Reaching out, she grabs my hand. "Let's go."

I sigh. I might as well just give up. If I don't go, she will only go by herself. "We're only going to look at it." I try to wear the same face my daddy does when he's warning me about something.

"You shouldn't worry so much." Viv links her fingers in mine as she leads me toward the door. Her palm is warm against my skin, and it makes me happy. "We're kids. We're supposed to be naughty." Her eyes twinkle, and I'm smiling as we run quietly down the hallway, past the door where Beth is giggling on the phone to her boyfriend, and around the corner toward the side door that leads outside.

My nose twitches as I smell the roses while we run across the grass. Lauren planted this huge garden with different colored roses a while ago. Viv and I helped her with some of it until Viv got bored and wanted to play on the swings and slide. I wanted to stay.

I love Vivien's mommy. She's so nice. She always gives me hugs and kisses and sneaks me chocolate and candy on the weekends. She is always telling my daddy it's not good enough.

I don't know what she means. Viv and I eavesdrop on their conversations sometimes, and my name comes up a lot. I feel sad if my daddy is telling Lauren I'm not a good boy. I try really hard, but Daddy always gets mad at me. I think that's why he works so much, and I don't see him during the week, and why he never wants to play with me when he's home on the weekends. I spend most of my time at Viv's house.

I wish I lived here all the time.

I wish Lauren and Jonathon were my mommy and daddy.

"Reeve!" Vivien tugs on my hand, and I blink as I stare up at the large oak trees. I don't even remember getting here. "Look how big it is!" Viv lets go of my hand, squealing and jumping up and down as we both look up. The treehouse is being built between two of the biggest trees in the garden and it looks ginormous. Lots of metal poles are pushed against the trees. There are planks of wood between the poles the men stand on when they are working. Earlier, when Viv and I were watching from her bedroom window, we saw the men climbing up and down with tools strapped to their belts. The roof is on and all but one side of the house is built.

"It looks awesome." Excitement bubbles up my throat. "It's going to be so cool."

"I'm going up." Viv races toward the poles at the side of the first tree.

"No." I run after her. "You can't go up there. You might fall."

"Don't be silly." She bats my hand away and lifts her foot onto the first pole. "I'll climb it like the men do."

"Please, Viv. Don't go up there. I don't want you to get hurt."

"Reeve." She turns around and flings her arms around me. "I won't get hurt. It will just be like rock climbing, and I never fall when I'm on the wall." Every Saturday, Viv's daddy,

Jonathon, takes us to the rock climbing wall at the local indoor climbing gym. It's fun, and we always race one another to the top. Viv hates it when I win, so I sometimes slow down on purpose. I don't mind losing to my best friend. I never want her to be sad or mad.

"You don't have a harness," I say into her hair as I hug her close.

"I don't need one." She gives me one last hug before starting to climb.

Another fluttery feeling starts in my chest, but it feels different than the last time. I wrap my arms around myself as Viv moves higher. "Be careful," I call out.

"I always am!" she shouts back. But that's not really the truth. If Viv wants to do something, she just does it. Sometimes, she does stupid things and gets into trouble.

I bite down on my lip and tip my head back as I watch her climb higher and higher. There's a weird taste in my mouth, and my stomach is all jumpy. I feel like I did that time I had a stomach bug and I puked everywhere.

Viv screams, and I watch in horror as she loses her footing and lets go of the metal poles. She is freefalling in the air. Her arms and legs are moving around, and I don't realize I'm screaming and shouting at first because I'm so scared I kinda zone out. Then I snap out of it and move. I have a sharp pain in my chest as I hold out my arms to catch her.

Viv lands heavily on top of me, and I lose my balance, falling to the ground at an awkward angle. But my arms are around her, tightening automatically so I won't let go. My ankle hurts, but I barely feel it because Vivien is screaming and holding her arm, and I'm more afraid than I've ever been.

"Viv." I sit up and keep my arms around her, ignoring the pain in my ankle. "What's wrong?" I ask, wiping the tears running down her face.

"My arm," she sobs. "It really hurts, Reeve." Her crying gets louder as she buries her face in my neck and leans into me.

"I told you it was dangerous." I wince as I attempt to stand and my ankle wobbles and shakes. I drop back to my butt, hugging my best friend.

"Make it stop, Reeve. It hurts real bad." Vivien's tears soak through my T-shirt, but I don't care. I only care that she's hurt. I should have made her stop; then none of this would have happened.

I rest my chin on her head. "Beth is coming," I say, spotting the nanny racing toward us with big eyes and pale skin. "She'll fix it."

"I'm scared." Viv cries. "Daddy is going to be so mad at me. Do you think I'll have to go to the hospital?"

I shrug. "Maybe."

"I need you." She holds me tight. "Don't leave me." Viv stares at me through big, watery hazel eyes as she clings to me with her good arm.

"I won't ever leave you, Viv. You're my best friend, and I'm staying until you're all better."

Dillon, the final book in the *All of Me Series* is available now in eBook, model paperback, alternate paperback and hardcover.

more pain. Until Jared rocks up to the art gallery where I work, with his fiancée in tow, and I'm drowning again.

Seeing him brings everything to the surface, so I flee. Placing distance between us again, I'm determined to put him behind me once and for all.

Then he reappears at my door, begging me for another chance.

I know I should turn him away.

Try telling that to my heart.

This angsty, new adult romance is a FREE full-length ebook, exclusively available to newsletter subscribers.

Type this link into your browser to claim your free copy:

https://bit.ly/TITMHFBB

OR

Scan this code to claim your free copy:

About the Author

Siobhan Davis™ is a *USA Today, Wall Street Journal*, and Amazon Top 5 bestselling romance author. **Siobhan** writes emotionally intense stories with swoon-worthy romance, complex characters, and tons of unexpected plot twists and turns that will have you flipping the pages beyond bedtime! She has sold over 2 million books, and her titles are translated into several languages.

Prior to becoming a full-time writer, Siobhan forged a successful corporate career in human resource management.

Siobhan currently lives with her husband in Cyprus while their two grown-up sons reside at the family home in Ireland.

You can connect with Siobhan in the following ways:

Website: www.siobhandavis.com
Facebook: AuthorSiobhanDavis
Instagram: @siobhandavisauthor
Tiktok: @siobhandavisauthor
Email: siobhan@siobhandavis.com

Books By Siobhan Davis

NEW ADULT ROMANCE SERIES

The Kennedy Boys® Series
Rydeville Elite Series
All of Me Series
Forever Love Duet
The One I Want Duet

NEW ADULT ROMANCE STAND-ALONES

Inseparable
Incognito
Still Falling for You
Holding on to Forever
Always Meant to Be
Tell It to My Heart
*Never Stopped Loving You**

REVERSE HAREM

Sainthood Series
Dirty Crazy Bad Duet
Surviving Amber Springs (stand-alone)
Alinthia Series

DARK ROMANCE - MAZZONE MAFIA

Condemned to Love
Forbidden to Love
Scared to Love
Vengeance of a Mafia Queen
Cold King of New York (The Accardi Twins #1)
Cold King of New York (The Accardi Twins #2)
Taking What's Mine
*Protecting What's Mine**

YA SCI-FI & PARANORMAL ROMANCE

Saven Series
*Broken World Series^*

---

*Coming 2025
^Previously the *True Calling Series*

www.siobhandavis.com